Amy Cross is the author of more than 100 horror, paranormal, fantasy and thriller novels.

OTHER TITLES
BY AMY CROSS INCLUDE

B&B

AMY CROSS

First published by Dark Season Books,
United Kingdom, 2017

Copyright © 2017 Amy Cross

ISBN: 9781520698496

Also available in e-book format.

www.amycross.com

CONTENTS

B&B

CHAPTER ONE

THERE'S SO MUCH SNOW in the air tonight, I can barely breathe.

Realizing that there's no sign of anyone answering the door, I clamber back up the icy steps and knock again. It's getting late and I really need a room for the night, just one night so I can decide where to go next, and this isn't the weather to start traipsing about the city. Climbing back down the steps, I look along the curving street and see Canterbury Cathedral in the distance, lit against the pitch-black sky as it towers high above the higgledy-piggledy buildings. The scene is so peaceful and calm, and the only sound is the gentle rustle of snow falling all around.

It's almost hypnotic.

Finally, figuring that nobody is going to answer the door, I reach down and grab the handle of my suitcase, dragging it around in the snow so I can set off along the street in search of somewhere else to stay. I'm freezing, and I need a warm bed so I can stop shivering and start figuring out what to do tomorrow. I've been running for long enough now; I need to make a decision about the future. Unfortunately, I called every other B&B in the city already and found they were all full, and now no-one's answering either the door or the phone at this one. I guess maybe I'll just have to sleep at the train station and hope I don't freeze.

And then tomorrow, I'll -

Suddenly I hear footsteps behind the B&B's blue door. I turn and look up, just as the door shudders and swings open. To my surprise, a woman emerges wearing a floral-patterned night-gown. She stops, staring at me with wild eyes that are barely visible through two holes in her bandages. Her entire head is swathed in clean white strips of cloth, as if she's some kind of burn victim, and she seems kinda startled by the sight of me. For several seconds, she simply watches me from the top of the steps, as if I'm the strangest, most surprising thing she's ever encountered in her life.

And still the snow falls. Maybe it's even heavier and faster than before, as if it's trying to bury me.

"Sorry," I say finally, figuring I have to be the first one to speak, "is this -"

Above me, there's a sudden creaking sound. I look up and see an old wooden sign for the Castle Crown B&B swinging gently in the late-night breeze. Snow has collected on the sign's edges, freezing against the wood.

"Do you have any rooms available?" I ask, turning back to look at the bandaged woman. "I know it's late. I tried calling from the phone-box at the station, but no-one answered. All the other B&B numbers I tried were full, so I figured..."

My voice trails off. I don't know what's wrong with this woman, but she seems utterly shocked by my presence. In fact, I'm starting to wonder if she's even the owner. I mean, I know it's a little late to be knocking, but she shouldn't be *this* surprised. If you run a B&B, you've gotta expect that sometimes -

Suddenly she slams the door shut, leaving me out alone on the street.

"Huh," I mutter. "Okay."

I wait.

Silence.

"I guess not, then," I say with a sigh. "I'll just -"

Suddenly the door swings back open, and the bandaged woman once again stares out at me. Maybe she thought I'd have vanished in a puff of smoke.

"I don't want to cause any trouble," I tell her, glancing at the window in case I missed a 'No Vacancies' sign. "I really just wanted to see if you had any rooms available for the night. I'm just kinda passing through, that's all. But if you don't have any vacancies, then..."

Again, I'm not quite sure how to continue. With snow still falling all around, I feel as if I'm only going to find it harder and harder to keep dragging my suitcase through the Canterbury streets, and it's already almost 10pm now. I need to find a room somewhere before it becomes impossible to get about, or I really *will* end up on a bench at the station. But if that's how things are gonna go tonight, then I guess I have no choice.

"Okay, then," I add, forcing a smile. "Sorry to disturb you. I'll try somewhere else."

With that, I turn and start pulling my suitcase along.

"Wait!" a rasping voice calls out suddenly.

I stop and turn back to see that the bandaged woman is still watching me from the doorway. I think the voice came from her, but it's hard to be sure.

"Come in," she continues, her voice sounding damaged and scratchy. There's a slit on the front of her bandages, but it's still not easy to hear what she's saying. Nevertheless, she gestures for me to follow her as she slips back into the darkness of the hallway, so I guess she must have an available room after all.

I glance both ways along the street, just in case by some miracle I spot another B&B I can try, and then I haul my suitcase to the foot of the steps. The damn thing is incredibly heavy and my arms ache as I start bumping it up to the doorway, and the process isn't helped by the fact that ice has started to form on the steps, forcing me to keep one hand on the railing. Finally, however, I manage to drag myself and the case through the doorway and into the narrow, high-ceilinged hallway, and I'm immediately struck by a rather fusty smell.

This place is old. Like, really old. I don't think it's been done up in... Well, let's be charitable and say *decades*. Still, beggars can't be choosers, and the place one very important thing going for it: nobody will ever think to look for me here. I can hide, even if it's just for one more night.

There's an open door to the left, and I can hear

someone shuffling about in there. Once my suitcase is safely inside, I swing the door shut and then I make my way to the door, where I find that the bandaged woman is rifling through a desk as if she's desperately searching for something. She seems almost panicked. For a moment, she almost seems to have forgotten that I'm here, but finally she glances in my direction. She stares at me with those same fearful eyes, and then she mutters something under her breath before leaving the desk and coming to the office door. She stops again, watching me with a hint of suspicion, but the holes in her bandages are so small that I can barely see her eyes properly at all. Something about this entire situation is making me feel pretty uncomfortable, and I'm starting to feel very glad that I'm only staying one night. If I had any other options, I'd be outta here already.

When I glance at the hooks on the wall, I see that there's only one key. I guess that means the other eleven rooms are all occupied for the night.

"So how much is it?" I ask, hoping to get the process started. I just want to get to bed and sleep on my next move. Everything will feel clearer in the morning. "A room, I mean. I don't want to put you out, but I'm kinda in a bind. I didn't expect to be coming here today, and then I didn't have time to call ahead, and I don't have a phone with me. It's kind of a funny story how I ended up here, I actually -"

Stopping suddenly, I realize that she probably doesn't want to know. Besides, I'd be lying anyway. It's not like I can tell her the truth. She'd call the police.

I reach into my pocket and carefully feel the wad

of money. I don't want to pull the whole pile out, in case I give her any ideas about bumping up the price, so I count off a few notes and then slip them out.

"I'll be paying cash," I tell her, hoping not to arouse suspicion.

Again I wait for her to say something, but again she seems shocked by the sight of me. I'm starting to wonder if she's drunk or high. Or crazy. Or all three.

"You *are* the owner, right?" I continue, unable to shake a sense of unease. "I just want a room, somewhere to sleep. I'm not fussy, but..."

I wait.

Nothing.

She simply stares at me.

"Okay, then," I say finally, realizing that this has gone beyond awkward and has turned into an extremely weird situation, "maybe I really *should* get going. I'm sure I can find another B&B, and if not I can always try to get the last train to London, or I can sleep at the station and leave in the morning." I take a step back. "I'll just be on my way and leave you in peace."

With that, I turn and head to the door.

"No!" the woman gasps suddenly. "Wait!"

Stopping, I turn back to her.

She reaches up and unhooks something, and then she swings down a section of wood that forms a makeshift counter in the doorway. Her hands are trembling, but at least now she actually seems to understand what I want, and I watch as she grabs some kind of printed form and a pen. She mumbles something under her bandages as she scribbles some details onto the form, but she stops halfway and slides the piece of paper away, letting it fall behind her to the floor.

"Are you okay?" I ask. "Is this a bad time? I just -"

"Room four," she mutters, slipping a key from the hook. She stares down at the key for a moment, as if she's a little indecisive. "I suppose," she adds. "Yeah. I guess you should take room four. It's the only one that's..."

Her voice trails off.

"It's the only one that's free," she continues finally, her voice filled with a hint of wonder.

"And how much is that?" I ask.

Again, she hesitates. "What?"

"How much is a room for the night?"

"Oh." She seems genuinely confused by the question, as if nobody has ever asked before. "The usual," she adds finally. "What was it? Forty-five? Sure. Forty-five pounds."

"That seems kinda cheap," I point out.

She stares at me for a moment, before shrugging.

"Okay." I count out the money from my little handful and set it on the counter. I'm still not sure I really want to stay here at all, and I'm starting to think a bench at the station might be less trouble. Still, I guess I'm here now. "And that includes breakfast?"

Again, she seems confused by the question.

"I suppose it does, yeah," she says, clearly in something of a daze. "Sure."

"My name's Bobbie," I reply, hoping to get things back on-track. "Roberta, actually, but people call me Bobbie. Don't you need to take my details?"

"Details?"

"So I can stay the night?"

She stares at me, and a moment later I hear a loud gulping sound from beneath the bandages.

"Roberta Simmons," I continue, taking my wallet from my pocket and slipping out my provisional license, before holding it up for her to see. I figure I should offer a little information now, rather than have her demand more later. So long as she doesn't run it by the police or ask to keep credit card details on file, I should be fine.

Outside, the wind is really howling.

Suddenly the woman snatches the license from my hand and turns so she can see it better in the light. Her hands are still trembling and she seems absolutely mesmerized for a moment as she looks at my details. In fact, this woman seems so confused and surprised by everything, and I'm more and more convinced that she's not right in the head. Either she has some kind of issue, or maybe there are noxious fumes in the building, or -

"Okay," she says suddenly, setting the license on the counter. "Fine. Okay. I get it."

"Sorry?" I ask, taking the license and sliding it back into my wallet.

She stares at me for a moment longer, and then she slowly starts nodding. "Okay," she adds. "Sure."

"Sure what?"

"Sure... Sure you can have the room. Why not, right?"

"Thank you," I reply as she raises the counter

and steps through to join me in the hallway. She still seems surprised somehow by my arrival, but at least she's apparently decided it's okay for me to stay. Even if I'm having second thoughts about that myself. "Like I said," I continue, "it's just for one night. To be honest, my plans are pretty fluid and it was kinda last-minute for me to come to Canterbury at all. I mean, this morning I didn't even..."

Sighing, I remind myself that she probably *really* doesn't care. Besides, the more I jabber on, the more like I am to trip myself up in a lie.

"I'll show you to your room," she mumbles from beneath the bandages, still holding the key in her shaking hands. After a moment, she turns and shuffles to the stairs, and I notice for the first time that she's barefoot and limping slightly.

"Thank you," I mutter, lugging my suitcase after her.

The stairs are steep and narrow, and they twist around on themselves halfway up. My suitcase feels heavier than ever; I've dragged it around all day, but now these final few meters are real agony. I'm already kinda out of breath, and I can't help noticing that the woman keeps glancing over her shoulder at me as she leads the way, almost as if she half-expects me to suddenly disappear.

Halfway up the stairs, there's a large plant in a pot. I don't know exactly what type it is, but the leaves are long and look a little spiky, with yellow tints at the green edges.

"Nice plant," I say, trying to make conversation.

She stops and looks down at the plant for a moment. "Yeah, you'd think so," she mutters bitterly, giving the pot a gentle kick before turning and continuing her march up to the next floor.

I stare at the plant, wondering what it could have done to earn such displeasure, but I quickly realize that there's no point worrying too much. Whatever's going on in this place, I just need to get my head down for the night and then leave first thing in the morning. And by the time I leave, I have to know where I'm going. I've put off the big decision long enough. Home isn't an option, but I'm not sure London's such a great idea either. I need a better plan.

My arms are aching, but I tighten my grip on the suitcase and then focus on bumping it the rest of the way up the stairs, while trying not to make too much noise in case I wake the other guests.

When I get to the top, I see that the bandaged woman is at the far side of the landing, already using the key to open one of the doors.

"You have a really nice place here," I tell her, trying to sound positive despite the discolored walls, weird paintings and strange smell. I drag my suitcase across the landing and into room four, where I find that the bandaged woman is standing with her back to the wall. If I didn't know better, I'd think she's actually a little afraid of me.

The room is small and basic, and it smells pretty damp, but it sure beats sleeping at the train station. Right now, the bed's the only thing that matters. I'm exhausted.

"Thank you so much for letting me stay," I say

as I set the suitcase down. My arms are aching worse than ever, and I'm still a little out of breath as I head over to the window and look out. At first, all I see is the reflection of the room's interior, but after a moment I realize the window overlooks a long, dark alley that runs behind the B&B. This house might be strange, and the landlady might be even stranger, but I'm still glad I'm not out there in this weather. A girl could freeze to death on a night like this.

Suddenly the woman mumbles something beneath her bandages.

I turn to her. "I'm sorry, what was -"

"Nothing," she says quickly, and now she seems even more frightened. "Ignore me. I didn't say anything."

"Okay," I continue, "but -"

She mumbles something else, and then she tosses the key onto the bed before heading to the door.

"What time is breakfast?" I ask.

Again, her voice is hard to make out, but I think she says something about breakfast being between seven and ten. To be honest, although I know I'll be hungry in the morning, I'm already starting to think that this B&B is way too weird for me to even want to *try* the breakfast. I saw a cafe down the street, so I can just go there for something to eat tomorrow while I'm heading to the train station.

Making my way over to the open door, I find that the woman is now loitering on the hallway, still staring at me.

"I think I just need to get to sleep," I tell her,

placing a hand on the edge of the door, ready to swing it shut. "I'm going to go to bed."

"Of course you are," she replies.

"I'm sorry?"

She shrugs, causing her bandages to rustle in the process.

"We have food in the basement," she adds. "Late-night snacks, that kind of thing. There's a tea and coffee machine. Sometimes people..."

Her voice trails off.

"You get the idea," she mumbles. "There are biscuits too."

"Is that the bathroom?" I ask, spotting a glass-paneled door behind her.

She turns and looks at it for a moment, before turning back to me and nodding. Again, her bandages rustle.

"Okay, thanks," I continue, forcing another smile. I wait a moment, hoping she'll take the cue and go back downstairs, but finally I realize she seems content to simply stand out there on the landing and watch me. "Goodnight, then," I add, before gently swinging the door shut.

I wait.

Silence.

Thank God that's over, although after a moment I realize I haven't heard her move anywhere, which means she might actually still be out there, just staring at my door. This is quite possibly the weirdest situation I've ever been in, in my whole life. I don't want to pull the door open again and check, so I stay completely still and listen, hoping against hope that I'll hear her walking away. The thought of her eyes still fixed on the door, staring out from behind her bandages, makes me feel extremely uneasy. Finally, figuring that I can't just go to bed without making sure she's gone, I crouch down and peer through the keyhole.

She's there.

Of course she is.

After a moment, however, she turns and hurries away, and I hear her rushing back down the stairs. A few seconds later, I hear a door slamming shut on the ground floor, which I guess means she must have retired to her little office to sleep or be weird or do whatever else she does in that room of hers.

I wait, and now the B&B is silent again.

In fact, it's so quiet, I could almost believe there are no other guests.

Stepping back from the door, I breathe a sigh of relief. This is what I needed. Tonight's the night I finally make a decision. I reach into my pocket and pull out the wad of money, and I count the notes as I head over to the bed. Slipping out of my jacket, I unzip the pockets on either side and take out the main wads, and I spend a couple of minutes making absolutely sure that I've kept track of my spending today. Once that nightly ritual is done and dusted, I divide the wads into their standard piles and put them where they belong, and then I unzip the suitcase and pull the lid open.

After moving my neatly-folded clothes aside, I check that the rest of the money is still sealed inside the Tesco bags, and then I take out the cloth satchel and unbutton it at one end. Sure enough, the rest of the money is still in its little bundles, completely untouched. I could count it again, of course, but I force myself to accept that everything's fine. I still have more than 95% of the cash, and so far I've used even less each day than I expected. I'm beating my budget. Then again, I know I shouldn't let myself get too comfortable. This can't last forever and I need a better plan.

And I need it by the time I wake up in the morning. Hopefully I can sleep on things and come up with something. I have to.

As I zip the suitcase shut again, I feel as if I just want to get my aching bones into bed. I've been waiting all day for this moment, and now the crisp white sheets are ready for me. I've been promising myself that tonight I'll figure out what to do, and that tomorrow morning I'll have a whole new plan. All I have to do is get undressed, climb into bed, and figure it all out.

I stand completely still, staring at the sheets.

What am I waiting for?

Sniffing the air, I suddenly realize that I'm pretty sweaty. In fact, I think I can actually smell my armpits, and I'd kinda like to get clean before I slide into these fresh sheets. I can get into bed after I've showered and there'll be plenty of time to come up with a plan. I just need to shower first. Even though I'm exhausted, I reach back into the suitcase and retrieve my toiletry bag, and then I grab the towels that have been left folded neatly on the bottom of the bed. I'll just go use the bathroom and take a quick shower, and then I can climb into this big clean bed and try to think of a plan, and then I can get some sleep.

And in the morning, I'll have a plan. And then -

Wait, am I just delaying?

I'm delaying.

I should get into bed and come up with a new plan.

Then again, it *does* make sense to take a shower first.

For a moment, I feel a flurry of panic in my chest. Real fear.

No, I'm not delaying.

I'm just gonna have a shower, and *then* I'll come up with a new plan. That makes total sense.

After making sure that I've got the key with me, I carry my stuff out to the empty landing. The light is off in the bathroom, so I figure I won't be disturbed. Turning, I pull the door shut and make doubly sure that it's locked, and then I head over toward the bathroom.

Stopping suddenly, I see that the bathroom light is now on. Not only that, but there's a woman standing outside the door, wearing a thick white dressing gown and holding a rolled-up towel in her hands. Turning to look at me, she stares for a moment before a big grin spreads across her lips.

"Well there you are, honey!" she says, patting a patch of floral wallpaper next to her. "Come on, quick! Get in line!"

CHAPTER TWO

"I'M SORRY," I STAMMER, trying not to look too startled, "I thought..."

Before I can finish, I hear the sound of someone splashing in the bath. I'm not entirely sure how, but in the blink of an eye it seems that not only is the bathroom occupied, but there's also someone waiting to go in next. Still, at least now I know there *are* other guests here at the B&B tonight.

"I can do this in the morning," I continue, "I just -"

"Nonsense," the woman says, as her smile grows. She's older than me, maybe in her late thirties or even early forties, but her smile seems very genuine and she has that kinda happy-go-lucky look about her that I've always envied in other people. She looks like she smiles without having to think about it first. "Come on," she adds, "don't fret, I won't be long in there. And trust me, I've been staying here long enough by now to know

16

that there's *never* not a queue. If you wanna get into that bathroom any time in the next twenty-four hours, you'd better get your butt over here and stake your spot. Otherwise, you'll just have to stink!"

I open my mouth to reply, but I'm honestly not quite sure what to say.

"Oh, look at you," she laughs. "Like a deer in the headlights. It's okay, I won't bite. I just came out to freshen up before bed, while my husband dozes in our room. I don't mean to complain, but I think it's just a little bad that there are twelve bedrooms in this place but only one bathroom. You should see the rush in the mornings. Everyone's in a hurry, trying to get in and pee and brush their teeth." She lets out a long, rather theatrical sigh. "Still, I guess that's progress for you. Back in the day, this place was run much better, it was all -"

She pauses, and then she smiles.

"Well, I don't want to badmouth anyone," she adds, "but between you and me, this B&B has rather gone downhill since the old days. I mean, look at the place, it's not exactly looking its best!" She slaps the wall. "Now come over here and claim your spot before somebody else comes and jumps in ahead of you. My name's Jude, by the way. I didn't catch yours."

She waits expectantly, and I quickly realize that I can't just shrink away.

"Bobbie," I say cautiously. "Roberta, but... People call me Bobbie."

"Well come on then, Bobbie," she continues, tapping the wall again. "We're British. Let's queue!"

I really just want to go back into my room, but I also need to use the toilet and I guess I should probably get in line. Heading across the landing, with my towels and toiletry bag clutched in my hands, I force a smile as I realize that this Jude woman seems to be watching my every move. I guess I'm just letting my usual unease get the better of me, so I lean back against the wall and try to act normal. After a moment, I find myself staring at the window on the far side of the landing, and watching as snow falls harder than ever.

"Are you okay there, honey?" Jude asks finally.

I turn to her.

"Oh, your face," she continues, evidently finding me pretty amusing. "What's up? First time away from home by yourself?"

"No," I reply quickly. Maybe *too* quickly. "I mean -"

"Are you all alone tonight," she continues, "or are you with your parents? Or do you have a hunky boyfriend hidden away in your room?"

"I'm alone," I stammer, although I quickly look down at my feet as I realize I might be about to blush. I hate the way I blush so easily.

In the bathroom, someone is still splashing about in the bath, and maybe even humming very quietly.

"Well, I envy you," Jude continues. "Sorta. Kinda. It must be nice to be free."

I take a deep breath. If only she knew.

"Then again," she adds, "I wouldn't trade my husband in for anyone else in the world. He's the kinda guy you can rely on, you know? Ever had a boyfriend like that?"

I shake my head.

"There's a lot to be said for dependability," she mutters. "You want a solid man, not someone who fades away at important moments. Plus, with the world the way it is, a woman can't really afford to be out alone. Especially not here. Especially not now. Canterbury's such a lovely city, but you wouldn't catch me walking the streets after dark, not by myself. It's just not safe."

I turn to her, confident now that any blushing is over.

"It seems nice to me," I tell her, feeling slightly proud of myself for managing to sustain a normal conversation.

"Are you insane?" she asks.

I swallow hard. That didn't go well.

"Did you hear that?" she asks suddenly, turning and looking toward the window.

I listen, but all I hear is the sound of someone still splashing about in the bath.

"You heard it, right?" she continues, with a hint of fear in her voice. "Footsteps!"

"I'm sorry?"

"Maybe I'm going crazy," she mutters, "but -"

She stops again, and this time I think maybe I *did* hear someone outside.

"You heard them that time, right?" Jude asks. "Come on, you're not deaf. I know you heard what I heard."

She steps past me and heads over to the window, where she stops for a moment and looks out at the snow.

Whoever's in the bathroom, their humming is a little louder now.

"Don't let the pretty cathedral fool you," Jude says finally as she looks out at the street. "I know it's fashionable for young women these days to wanna prove themselves, to act all tough, but take my advice. Don't risk it. All the stories you've heard about this place are true. All of them. Maybe there's been some exaggeration in the media. Maybe. But I've been here long enough to overhear a lot of talk, and from what I hear the basics of it all are true. This really is a city you don't wanna go wandering around in, especially late at night in the dark. Especially when it's snowing."

"I kind of like the snow," I tell her.

"Sure. Until you bleed all over it. Until you get your throat slit open."

I pause, convinced that I must have heard her wrong. "I beg your pardon?" I ask finally.

She turns to me. "You *do* know about it all, right?" she asks cautiously. "Please, tell me you know the story about what's going on here. About why you shouldn't go out at night. I mean, come on, it might look like a picture postcard out there but..."

Her voice trails off.

"Well, stone the crows," she adds after a moment, "you really *don't* know, do you?"

"This is my first time in Canterbury," I tell her. "I just got off the train here because..."

Now it's my turn to fall silent. I can't possibly explain my thought process. This woman seems nice, but she'd hate me if she knew what I'd done.

"And you haven't been watching the news?"

"Not really," I reply.

In fact, I've been specifically *avoiding* the news. The last thing I want to see is my own face being broadcast.

"Oh, honey." She rolls her eyes. "It's *him*, you know? The guy with the weather fixation."

I wait for her to continue. "I'm sorry," I say finally, "but I have no idea what you're talking about."

She smiles as she turns and looks back out the window.

"They call him the Snowman," she says after a moment.

"The Snowman?"

"On account of how he only kills when it's snowing outside."

I stare at her for a moment, wondering whether she's serious.

"It's all true," she continues. "No-one knows who he is or why he does it, but the stories are definitely true. He doesn't seem to ever kill any other time, but whenever it snows in this city, he goes out and takes himself another victim. Regular as clockwork."

I watch as snow drifts past the window, and after a moment I look down toward the dark alley below.

"Some people think it's because of a psychological problem," she adds. "Like, maybe something bad happened to him one year when it was snowing, and now he's tortured by the memory of it all. Other people think maybe he uses the snow somehow, like it's part of a ritual." She pauses. "But that's not what it is. Oh no. He just can't stand all the white."

I wait for her to continue, but after a few seconds I realize that maybe she thinks she's explained enough.

"All the white?" I ask cautiously.

"Look at it," she continues. "All that snow, all settled everywhere. I think when he sees everything all white, he feels this urge to splatter it with red." She sniffs, almost as if she's smelling something strong and powerful. "I think every time there's a blanket of snow on the city, he's compelled to go out there and paint on that big, white canvas. I think he likes the way blood splatters on snow, and the way it soaks into the little ice crystals. To be perfectly honest with you, I actually kinda understand his point of view. The desire to take all that white and make it dirty somehow. To spill blood and watch as it sinks into the cold, wet snow, melting it a little before the snow eventually makes the blood freeze." She shudders. "Poor boy. I definitely understand his need. Don't you?"

I stare at the snow for a moment longer, before realizing that she's turning to look at me.

I turn to her.

"I'm not sure about that," I stammer cautiously. "It sounds kinda nuts."

She eyes me with a certain hint of disdain. "Well that's a matter of opinion," she points out finally.

I nod. "It sure is."

Turning, I look out the window again. The alley behind the B&B certainly looks dark and imposing, even with a thick blanket of snow. There's a radiator next to my feet, filling the landing with warm air, but when I lean closer to the window I realize the glass is ice-cold. For a moment, I'm mesmerized by the sight of the dark alley, and by the thought that anyone could want to disturb such a beautiful scene by doing something violent and horrific.

"Maybe there was no-one there," Jude continues after a moment. "I guess we're all a little jumpy, right? I mean, it's not like we could be lucky enough to see the Snowman walk past just as we happen to be looking out. That'd be crazy."

"Lucky?" I ask, surprised by her choice of words.

"You know what I mean. Coincidental."

"I guess not."

The alley certainly looks dark right now, and there's no sign of any footprints in the snow. In fact, it's hard to believe that anyone has been out there for quite some time.

"Imagine living your life," Jude continues, "and just trying to be an ordinary citizen. Trying to be a good boy. And then you glance outside and see that it's snowing, and you realize you're gonna have to kill again. He's murdered several people over the past thirty years, all of them on snowy days. Imagine the weather doing that to you. It's almost like he has no control, except obviously he *does* have control. That must be what makes it so tantalizing."

I force a smile, even though I'm not entirely sure I agree with her.

"Is that mud?"

I flinch as I feel her finger against the side of my

neck. Pulling away, I see that she's scraped some mud from behind my ear.

"Sorry," she adds, wiping the mud on her towel. "I just saw it, that's all. How did it get there?"

"Long day," I reply.

"Well," she continues with a grin, "I guess you really *do* need a wash. Maybe more than I do."

She pauses, eyeing me with a hint of caution, as if she's lost in thought. She's still smiling, but it's a forgotten smile, one that has been left on her face long after the impulse has passed.

"I tell you what I'm gonna do," she says finally, taking a step back. "I'm gonna let you have the bathroom."

"Oh, no, really that's -"

"I've already decided!" she adds, before biting her bottom lip for a moment. "You're clearly in more need than I am, and it's a long night. I can come back out at two, three, even four in the morning and perform all my ablutions. I couldn't, in all good conscience, enjoy myself if I knew you were out here all caked in mud and dirty. Besides, sometimes I find the bathroom a little sad. I don't wanna be in there right now."

"I'm not really *caked* in mud," I point out, reaching up and checking that there's no more behind my ear. I don't even know where the first spot came from.

"Have fun," she says, unlocking the door to room three and stepping inside. "I'm sure we can all enjoy the bathroom, so long as we just cooperate. There's no need for anyone to be pushing and shoving. Just promise you won't complain if you hear me singing in the bath during the night. I can get a little loud sometimes, but that's just my way. If you can't handle me at my worst, you sure as hell don't deserve me at my best. Am I right, or am I right?"

She smiles, before glancing at the window. The snow seems to make her sad, and I swear there are tears in her eyes now.

"Poor boy," she adds finally. "Out there, compelled to kill just because of the weather. Poor, poor boy."

With that, she swings the door shut, leaving me standing all alone on the landing.

"Huh," I mutter, feeling more than a little shell-shocked. After a moment, I look back over at the window and watch as snow continues to fall, and then I glance at the bathroom door.

I blink.

And now the door is open.

I swear, the whole time I was talking to Jude, the bathroom door was shut. I even heard someone splashing about in there, but now the door is a couple of inches ajar. The light is still on, but there's nothing else to suggest that anyone is in there.

I pause, considering whether or not I should go and knock, but finally I lean back against the wall. There's no way anyone came out when I wasn't looking, so I guess whoever's in there is just finishing up.

Several minutes tick past, with not a sound in the entire B&B. The whole place seems completely still and lifeless. Even the bathroom.

I glance at the door again.

A normal person would knock. A normal person would start coughing loudly, to hurry the occupant along. A normal person wouldn't just stand here like a moron, *hoping* to get into the bathroom.

Still, I should probably just wait. There's no harm in being patient.

Suddenly spotting movement, I turn and see that someone is coming down the stairs from the floor above. A woman steps into view, with long hair hanging down almost to her waist. She makes no sound, not even as her bare feet pad against the thick carpet, but then she stops as soon as she sees me. For a moment, she seems utterly startled by my presence, and I can't help noticing that she looks very pale, with ashen grayish skin and ice-white eyes. And then, just as quietly as she came down, she starts slowly backing up the stairs again.

"I'm just waiting for the bathroom," I tell her, forcing a smile. "I won't be long."

Keeping her eyes fixed on me, she withdraws into the shadows at the top of the stairs, and then she's gone.

"I promise," I add forlornly, but it's too late. I guess she's not the talkative type.

So I wait again.

And I wait.

And I wait.

I don't know how much time passes, but it must be at least ten minutes. I glance at the door a couple more times, hoping to spot some hint of movement, but there's absolutely nothing. More and more, I'm starting to think that maybe someone *did* come out after all, and somehow I just missed them.

This is silly.

I can't just stand here all night like this, queuing without even know if I'm waiting for anyone. No matter how reluctant I might be to cause trouble, I finally head closer to the door, while still listening out for any hint of movement.

"Hello?" I call out tentatively. "Is anyone in there?"

By the time I reach the door, there's still no answer.

I know gently.

"Hello?"

Silence.

"I'm gonna come in, okay?" I continue. "I'm just gonna open the door. Just be aware of that, okay?"

The last thing I want is to catch someone naked.

I take hold of the door, which thankfully creaks a little. Good. That's a little extra warning. Finally, with a tightening knot of anticipation in my chest, I start pushing the door open. I see the sink, with no-one there, and then I see that the shower cubicle is also empty. Pushing the door further, I see the window and towel rack, and still there's no sign of anyone, and finally I get the door all the way open and I see the bath.

It's empty.

I breathe a sigh of relief.

Of course it's empty.

I turn and push the door shut, and then I turn back toward the sink.

And I freeze.

Suddenly there's a woman sitting neck-deep in dark red water, staring at me.

I open my mouth to say something, but the words stick in my throat. It takes a moment before I recognize the woman, with her hair now wet and straggly, as Jude. There's no way she could have made it from her bedroom back into the bathroom without going straight past me, not unless there's some hidden door that I never noticed before. And yet here she is, right in front of me, so obviously she made it in here somehow.

"Sorry," she says, with a somewhat dreamy tone to her voice. "I didn't think I'd be disturbed this late at night. I promise I won't be much longer. I actually thought I'd be done by now, but it's taking a little more time."

All I can do is stare at her, and at the calm red surface of the bath water.

"I don't mean to be picky," she continues, "but would you mind waiting outside until I'm finished? I know it might sound foolish, but I'd like a little privacy for this."

Still frozen to the spot, I really don't know what I'm supposed to do next.

"Please?" she adds. "And shut the door once you're gone. I don't want anyone else walking in on me. Not during these final moments. I'd like a little peace."

I pause, before turning and heading back to the door. Once I'm out on the landing, I pull the door shut and stop again, staring down at the rich red carpet. I keep telling myself that I imagined that second encounter with Jude, or that I at least imagined the bloody water, but the image is burned into my mind and I can't force it out, not even when I squeeze my eyes shut. Once I open them again, I find myself still staring at the carpet. Sitting in the bath, Jude seemed so calm and peaceful, and so matter-of-fact about the whole situation. I must have misunderstood.

Yeah, that's it.

Whatever I thought was going on in there, I was wrong. I mean, it wouldn't be the first time I've gotten my social cues all mixed up.

Whatever's going on here, it's my fault.

I lean against the wall again, figuring I should just keep waiting, but the bathroom has once again fallen still and quiet. I can't think about anything other than the red water, and I'm starting to feel more and more convinced that the bath really *was* filled with blood. I always shy away from any kind of confrontation, but this time I figure that any normal person would go back in and make sure that Jude is okay. Besides, I didn't specifically ask her what she was doing,. What if something's wrong and I could help her? What if she's in trouble and I could save her life?

Taking a deep breath, I head back to the door and knock gently.

"Hello?" I whisper. "Are you... Are you okay in there?"

No reply.

"I just... I saw the water," I continue, "and I started thinking that maybe..."

I pause.

How should I phrase this? How do you ask

someone, politely, if they're committing suicide?

"Do you need help?" I ask finally. "Should I fetch someone or call someone or..."

I wait, but there's still no reply.

The last thing I want is to disturb her, but I'm worried she might have passed out. Reaching down, I rest my fingers on the door handle for a few seconds, weighing up the pros and cons of going back inside. I really, *really* hope that I'm just misunderstanding the whole situation. After a moment, realizing that I have to at least check on her one more time, I turn the handle and push the door open, and then I step back into the bathroom.

Jude is still in the bath, still staring at me.

"I really won't be much longer," she says calmly. "I know, it must seem like I'm taking forever. I'm a little surprised myself, but I suppose there's no rule book. If you could just wait outside until I'm done, that'd be grand."

I stare at the water for a moment.

"What are you..." I swallow hard. "What are you doing?"

"What am I *doing*?"

"What are you doing in there?"

"What does it look like?" she asks, as if it's the oddest question she's ever heard in her life. "I'm taking a bath."

"Yeah, but..."

My voice trails off. I'm starting to feel a rush of panic in my chest, and I think maybe I should just go get someone else to take care of this situation. After all, I've never been much of a people person.

"Life is so tiring," she says suddenly. "Don't you ever think that? Don't you ever feel like you've been worn down past the point where you can ever go on?"

I swallow again, but this time my throat is dry.

"And don't you ever feel like you've hit a brick wall?" she continues. "Like you're at the end of your tether, and nobody else understands, and you just feel an immense urge to retreat from the world? It's all just too much, too crushing, too destroying, and you're done with it. You want to go away and never have to face all the cruelty again."

I open my mouth to say something, but still I can't get any words out. All I can do, slowly, is back away to the door. Please don't let this be what it looks like. Please...

"It's too hard," she adds, with a hint of tears in her eyes now. "It's just too much. Too vicious. Too full of hate. I can't handle the world anymore."

I shake my head. "This isn't the answer," I tell her finally, figuring I should say *something*. "Please... I'm going to get help. I'm going to call an ambulance."

"An ambulance?"

"Of course," I reply, even though it's hard to believe she's even conscious after losing so much blood. "Just wait right here and -"

"Where else would I go?"

"I'll be right back," I add, turning to head out the door, "and -"

"Wait!" she says suddenly. "You don't think I'm -"

I turn back to her.

She stares at me for a moment, then she looks down at the red water, and then she turns to me again and smiles. A few seconds later, the smile becomes a laugh and she lifts her right arm out of the bath, revealing a ragged and torn wrist covered in criss-cross slices. Thick red blood is dribbling from the wound, and I can see hints of white bone deep in the gore.

With her other hand, Jude reaches up and starts tearing at the loose flesh, pulling it aside to reveal more of the bone.

"Well if he did it," she sneers, her voice filled with anger, "then why don't I get to do it too? I feel bad for the poor boy, but he'll just have to manage!"

"I'll get help," I stammer, turning to leave the room as she starts laughing. I fumble with the handle for a moment, before glancing back at her. "I'll -"

She's gone.

I stare at the empty bath, but there's no sign of Jude at all. Too shocked to even move, I simply stand completely still and wait for her to reappear, but it's as if she was never here to begin with. My mind is racing as I try to figure out exactly what just happened, but there's only one way in or out of the bathroom and I'm pretty damn sure she didn't come past me. Every explanation I come up with feels wrong, as if I'm hitting dead ends in my mind, and finally I come to the only possible conclusion.

It's impossible.

She can't have been here.

Which means the whole encounter was just in

my head. Am I crazy enough to start hallucinating people? I didn't think so, but I guess it's possible that the past few days have gotten to me in ways I never anticipated. Stepping back against the wall, I can't help staring a little longer at the bath, just in case she magically reappears, but as the seconds tick past I realize that she's really, truly gone. Or rather, she was never here in the first place.

I'm cracking up.

"You're cracking up," I whisper under my breath.

My heart is pounding, but I know I have to get myself back under control. I've been worried for a while that something like this might happen, that the stress would finally break something in my mind. It'd be so easy to panic and run, to grab my suitcase and leave the B&B far behind. I could tell myself that the place is haunted, and I could pretend that these strange apparitions come from the world around me. That wouldn't be true, though. Jude, at least while she was bleeding in the bath, came from my own mind.

I refuse to go crazy.

I want to go back to my room and lock the door, and hide away until morning, but after a moment I realize I should probably make use of the bathroom now that I actually have the place to myself. I'm strong, I'm tough, and I won't crumple at the first sign of madness. Pushing the door shut, I slide the lock across and then head over to the sink, where I set down my toiletry bag and towel.

Looking at my reflection in the mirror, I see that

I look much the same as I did this morning. I suppose that's a good thing. The day's events haven't taken too much of a toll just yet. I don't look crazy, but I *will* if I don't pull myself together.

I take a deep breath.

One night, that's all.

I have to stay sane for one more night. Taking another deep breath, I feel my heart slowing something closer to a normal pace. I close my eyes for a moment, counting slowly in an attempt to regain control. Finally, I open my eyes again.

And that's when I see it.

Something's in the bath. Something large. Something on its side at the bottom of the tub.

I continue to stare at the reflection, shocked by what looks like a naked, red-stained male body. It can't be that, of course. I know it can't. The bath was empty a moment ago, and there's no way anyone came into the room. This is just my mind trying again to trip me up.

And yet, as I continue to stare at the bath, I see that there really *is* a red-stained naked man at the bottom, curled away from me. He's not moving at all, not even shivering despite the coolness of the room. I tell myself that maybe this is some kind of trick, that perhaps he's just a very lifelike model, but something about the body's bloated, pocked flesh looks awfully real to me as I slowly turn away from the mirror and look directly at the bath.

The tub's white sides have been left light pink by sediment from the water, and there's a strong scent in the air, a hint of iron.

Blood.

"This isn't happening," I whisper. "It's not possible."

I close my eyes and wait a moment, before opening them again.

He's still there.

I close them again.

I wait longer.

I open them.

He's still there.

Taking a deep breath, I close my eyes for a third time.

"Go away," I whisper. "Go... away..."

I wait.

"Please," I add finally, before opening my eyes again.

He's still there. Of course he is.

Stepping closer to the bath, I lean over the figure until I can see the man's face. His eyes are closed, but the stubble around his chin looks very genuine and I can tell that he isn't breathing. He looks to be in his late fifties at the very least, and there's a faded green tattoo on his upper left arm, although I can't quite make out the lettering. Whatever's going on here, I know I should call the police, but at the same time I can't quite bring myself to do that. Then again, I could just go to the phone-box at the train station and give them an anonymous tip. That way, they could deal with whatever's happening here but I wouldn't have to get involved.

I *can't* get involved.

The police are already going to be looking for

me. The last thing I can afford is to start attracting their attention. Besides, I have to focus on the fact that no matter how real this man looks, he's most likely not here at all. My mind is simply playing tricks on me, and I *have* to get my thoughts straight.

I take a step back, figuring that -

Suddenly my bare feet slip in a puddle of bloody water. I let out a gasp, but I'm too late to steady myself and I fall back, crashing down to the floor and slamming the back of my head against the tiles with such force that everything immediately goes black.

CHAPTER THREE

"BOBBIE? BOBBIE, YOU CAN'T sleep here. Bobbie, wake up."

Opening my eyes, I'm immediately startled by the bright moonlight that's streaming through the window, casting net-curtain patterns across the bathroom ceiling. A moment later, Jude leans over me, still wearing her dressing gown and still clutching her towels and toiletry bag. There's a faint smile on her face, although she also seems a little concerned.

"Was something wrong with your bed?" she asks. "Some of them can be a little lumpy. He hasn't changed the mattresses in years. But you can't sleep in the bathroom, honey. Other people need to use it."

She checks her watch.

"It's midnight. Go to bed."

I stare at her for a moment, before suddenly remembering the man's body in the bath. Sitting bolt upright, I slam my head into the underside of the sink, and I immediately let out a gasp of pain.

"Watch yourself!" Jude continues, taking a step back. "Wow, that sounded like it hurt a *lot*! I hope you didn't crack your head open!"

Rubbing the sore patch, I get to my feet and look down into the bath, half-expecting to see the red-stained body. Instead, I see that not only is the body gone, but the entire bath and surrounding area appears to have been cleaned, and the smell of blood is gone too. I look over at the window, which remains shut with ice-crystals on the glass, and more snow is falling through the darkness outside. If anything, the weather just seems to be getting worse and worse. Nearby, the shower is still running after I turned it on. Finally, I turn to Jude.

"What's up, honey?" she asks. "You look like you've seen a ghost."

"Where is he?"

"Where's who?"

"The man!"

She furrows her brow. "What man?"

"The man you left in the bath last night."

She stares at me for a moment. "I don't have a clue what you're talking about, sweetie-pie," she says finally. "You didn't bang your head, did you?"

I stare at her, and it takes a moment before I'm able to remind myself that the man wasn't real. He was all in my head.

"Was there anyone else here when you came in just now?" I ask.

"In the bathroom? Of course not. It was just you, silly."

I look down at the bath again, but there's absolutely no sign that the man was ever here. Even the area around the plug-hole is clear of the red stain, although there are a few flecks of limescale. I honestly don't know how somebody could have cleaned the bath but left limescale behind, especially clean limescale that shows no sign of having been colored red. It's pretty clear that I hallucinated, probably due to lack of sleep.

"So are you done in here?" Jude asks brightly. "Sorry, I just really need to shower!"

I turn to her. "Can I see your wrists?"

She furrows her brow.

"Humor me," I continue.

She pauses, before holding her hands up to reveal a pair of clean, undamaged wrists.

"Huh," I whisper, realizing that this is all the evidence I need. I guess there's no doubt now. I really *am* losing my mind, in which case running away from the B&B would probably make things worse. I need to stick the night out here, no matter what.

***

I was planning to go straight to bed after my experience in the bathroom, but I'm starving and I figure I could use some of those biscuits that the landlady mentioned earlier. I run some deodorant across my armpits and then I head downstairs, where I locate another flight of steps that seems to lead down to the basement. I'm already halfway down when I realize I can hear voices coming from below, and I pause for a moment, feeling as if I should just go back to my room. After all, I *really* don't feel like talking to anyone right now.

"Oh hey," an elderly man says suddenly, limping out of the brightly-lit kitchen with a bowl of fruit in his hands. He stops and smiles at me. "Another guest for the feast, eh?"

I stare at him, feeling a little startled.

"We've been raiding the refrigerator," he continues with a grin. "It's become something of a tradition these past few nights. I keep telling myself we should stop, but these strawberries are just so yummy."

He pauses, as if he's waiting for me to reply, and then he turns and carries the berries through to join the other voices in the next room.

I hesitate, still convinced that I should go back to my room, before reminding myself that this is precisely the kind of anti-social behavior I've been meaning to stamp out. I have to be less scared of people, so I *need* to force myself to go through and at least fetch some tea and biscuits. It won't kill me to be slightly sociable, and I might even benefit from being around other, normal people. I take a deep breath and try to ignore the fear in my chest, and then I make my way across the hallway and over to the door.

The next room is a low-ceilinged little space with half a dozen tables neatly set out. There's an elderly couple sitting at the closest table, playing cards while nibbling potato chips from various bowls, while a younger girl – my age, or maybe even a few years younger, in her late teens – is sitting quietly and a little meekly behind them, reading a book. Another man, middle-aged and wearing a striking yellow and black checkered blazer, is sitting at a table in the middle of the room, watching the card game, and he grins at me as I mumble a greeting and head to the coffee machine on a table at the side of the room.

"We have another guest!" the middle-aged man says, evidently amused. "And at such a late hour, too! Still, it's always nice to welcome someone to our little shindig. As you might have noticed, my dear, we're enjoying something of a lock-in!"

He raises a finger to his lips.

"Don't make too much noise, though," he continues. "We don't want to wake the ghosts."

I manage to find a smile from somewhere. I hope it seems genuine.

"My little joke," he continues, getting to his feet and using a hand to smooth his slicked-back hair. Stepping closer, he extends the same hand for me to shake. "You must call me Lloyd. Do you want to know why?"

"Um..."

"Because it's my name, silly!" he continues, giggling at his own joke.

I force myself to shake his hand, which feels predictably greasy.

"Now," he adds, "I understand that it can feel very lonely to be the outsider in a group, but we're very welcoming and you'll soon feel right at home with us. Most of us have been staying here for... Well, for a little while now. Several nights, at least, as guests of the delightful Castle Crown Bed and Breakfast. Do you know, this place has been a home away from home for travelers since the middle of the last century?"

"That's nice," I reply.

"We're all just lonely pilgrims seeking room and board for a few nights," he continues, lowering his hands and placing them on his hips. "On a cold winter's eve, one doesn't want to be searching for lodgings, especially not when there's rumored to be a killer on the prowl." He turns and looks at the girl in the corner, who still has her nose in a book. "I've told Matilda over and over, she's *just* the kind of girl the Snowman would go after. Young, pretty, innocent, naive, defenseless. I dare say if he spotted her out and about, he wouldn't hesitate to gut her. I mean, look at her. The poor girl's style positively begs someone to drag her into a dark alley."

He watches her for a moment.

"Did you hear me?" he calls out suddenly. "Matilda? Did you hear what I just said?"

Again, she ignores him.

"You'd be dead in minutes," he continues, as if he's trying to goad her into a response. "No killer could resist you!"

A flicker of discomfort crosses the girl's face, and it's quite clear that she's heard every word Lloyd is saying, but she doesn't seem to want to acknowledge him. Instead, she pointedly turns to another page in her book. I can't entirely say I blame her.

"Then again," Lloyd continues, glancing back at me with a leering eye, "I suppose *you* might be his type too."

He looks me up and down for a moment.

"Yes," he mutters, "you really might."

"I just came to get something to eat," I reply, turning and taking a cup from the trolley. I drop a tea-bag into the cup, before examining the machine and seeing that there's only one nozzle for both coffee and water, which means the tea is going to taste a little weird. Still, I guess beggars can't be choosers, so I slip the tea under the nozzle and press the button for water.

Nothing happens.

"Give it a minute or two to catch up," Lloyd explains. "Major Denham asked it for water just now, so it rather needs to catch its breath. That's the thing about these old models. They can still do the job, but you have to let them rest in-between. Rather like older men."

I can hear a faint gurgling sound coming from deep inside the machine, so I guess it's at least thinking about giving me some water.

"Would you care to join the game?"

I turn to Lloyd.

"It might be more fun with you," he continues. "I wanted to play Onesies and Twosies, but Matilda's being a stick-in-the-mud as usual, but you could be the fourth hand. I promise you'll have a wonderful time! We're very friendly, and we're exceedingly welcoming when new people join our little group. I know Major and Mrs. Denham can seem rather frosty, but that's just their way with everyone. Don't worry if you haven't played it before. You'll soon get the hang of things."

"I'm fine, thank you," I tell him, desperately hoping that the machine will spit out my water soon. "I'm not really much of a game player."

"Nobody is until they give it a go!"

"It's very late," I point out.

"Of course, but how can anybody sleep on a night like this?" He leans past me and places a hand on the wall. "Feel that!"

"I'm sorry?"

"Feel the wall!"

Figuring I should be polite, I turn and put my hand close (but not too close) to his. "It's cold," I mutter, stating the obvious.

"Exactly! We're nice and warm in here, but outside it's another freezing, snowy night in the good city of Canterbury. And he's out there somewhere, you know. He's traipsing through the streets, looking for his next victim."

"Sure," I mutter.

"The Snowman," he continues. "Don't tell me you haven't heard of him."

"I've heard of him," I reply, before glancing at the coffee machine. It's taking so long to deliver a cupful of hot water, but I know it'd seem rude if I abandoned ship now. I wish I was one of those people who didn't mind seeming rude, especially around strangers.

"This is the perfect night for the Snowman," Lloyd explains. "Cold, snowy, deserted. He'll be out there somewhere in one of the dark streets, or lurking in one of the darker alleys. Everyone knows not to go out in these conditions. The police have issued warnings, and history speaks for itself, but you can bet that someone at some point will decide they can take the risk, and some slight young lady will venture out into the snow, trampling along an empty street, convinced that she'll be fine. But he'll find her, and he'll pursue her, and he won't even give her time to scream. And then in the morning, there'll be a corpse in the bloody snow."

He leans closer to me.

"Mark my words," he continues. "Somebody *will* die tonight. I even..."

He glances over his shoulder, as if to check that the elderly man and woman are still chatting away to one another, and then he leans ever closer to me.

"I even spotted him," he whispers. "I think so, anyway."

I wait for him to continue. "Spotted who?" I ask finally.

"Him! The Snowman! Tonight!"

"You did?"

"I was looking out through one of the windows," he adds conspiratorially, "at around quarter to eleven. I suppose I was feeling rather listless, and perhaps a little out-of-sorts. One gets that way sometimes, especially on a night like this when one fears a killer might be on the loose. And I just happened to be looking out at exactly quarter to midnight, while I was trying to decide whether or not to come downstairs tonight for another late-night session, and I saw someone hurrying right past the B&B! I didn't get any details, all I really spotted was the shadow of a figure, but there was definitely *somebody* out there!"

"Maybe it was just someone going about their business," I suggest, trying not to let him see that I can smell his coffee breath.

"We both know it was no such thing," he continues. "This particular figure was trying very hard to keep from being seen. Very, *very* hard. There's no doubt in my mind, it was the Snowman, out on the prowl again. I thought about calling the police, to tip them off, but it's not as if the information would really help them. They've been rather lackadaisical about catching him, to say the least."

"Still," I reply, "it wouldn't hurt to -"

"Anyone foolish enough to risk going out there," he adds, "deserves to get their warm guts ripped out and dropped onto the cold snow. Don't you think? It's a kind of natural selection. All the smart people are huddled in the warmth and safety of their homes. Or their B&B, in our case. I'll tell you one thing for free, young lady. You couldn't pay me to go outside tonight, not with all the money in the world or all the tea in China. Especially not if I was a pretty young lady such as yourself."

He glances over his shoulder.

"Or Matilda."

I wait for him to continue, while desperately hoping that he won't. Matilda looks extremely uncomfortable as she focuses on her book, and I feel as if I've stepped into the middle of something that's been brewing for quite a while.

Suddenly the coffee machine emits a loud clunking sound. I turn and look at the spout, but to my disappointment I see that only a dribble has come out.

"Turn it off and on again," Lloyd suggests.

I turn to him.

"Sometimes it works as a last resort." He steps

away from me and leans behind the machine. I hear a switch being flicked, and the machine's lights go dead, and then Lloyd hits the switch again and all the lights briefly blink green. "It'll still take a minute or two," he explains, "but at least you'll get your tea water at the end of it. And that's what you really want, isn't it?"

I force a smile. What I *really* want is to go up to my room, and I wish I'd never started messing with the machine in the first place. There's a pile of biscuits in a bowl, and I should have just grabbed a few of those and retreated. I suppose it's too late now, since I don't want to seem rude. It's typical of me to get myself into this kind of situation, though. All I want is a good night's sleep, and instead I'm stuck here talking to strangers and waiting for an ancient-looking coffee machine to finally give me water.

Suddenly I hear a buzzing sound.

"Maybe that's him!" Lloyd exclaims, unable to hide his excitement as he slips his phone from his pocket. "Maybe the Snowman has struck!"

I watch as he taps at the screen, and a moment later he rolls his eyes.

"Just another news article about him," he says with a sigh. "I have alerts set up, so I'm notified every time the Snowman is mentioned by a credible news site. Unfortunately, a lot of them are posting speculative guff tonight. I wish they'd keep the hashtags clear for *real* developments."

He taps a couple more times, before slipping his phone back into his pocket.

"This bally thing is clearly playing up," he

continues, tapping the top of the coffee machine, "but it *will* give you the water you want eventually. In the meantime, won't you at least sit with us? It'd be rude not to!"

He heads over to the table and pulls out a chair for me. I open my mouth to tell him I'm fine standing, but I guess I don't want to seem unfriendly. Besides, I'm still worried that I might start hallucinating again once I'm alone, so it might be better to at least wait while the machine starts working again.

I can hear howling wind outside as I head over to where the elderly man and woman are engrossed in their game.

"So I told him it's no way for an ambulance driver to behave," the woman is explaining as she peers at her cards. "I said to him, if someone *annoys* him, he needs to deal with it the proper way, rather than waiting 'til he bumps into her at the scene of an accident and... Well, it's not right what he did, is it? Although I've gotta admit, it gave me a good giggle. I'm going to hell for that, I am. Straight to hell in a handbag."

"Four of spades," the man mutters.

"No," she says quickly, before looking up at me. She stares at my face for a moment, and then a smile slowly creeps across her lips. "And what do we have here, eh? A new arrival?"

"I -"

Before I can say a word, I spot movement nearby, and I turn just in time to see the bandaged landlady stopping in the doorway. She looks somewhat flustered, with both her floral-patterned nightgown and her bandages appearing out-of-sorts. Behind her, the door to the boiler room is swinging shut. She quickly reaches up and adjusts the bandages, and then she fixes her nightgown until she looks a little more presentable, but she still seems utterly startled. I guess maybe that's just her default state.

"The coffee machine is still on the fritz," Lloyd tells her. "I tried turning it off and on again. Whatever you did, it hasn't made a spot of difference."

She looks over at him for a moment, and then she turns to the machine.

"You want to get that thing fixed," he continues.

She seems frozen to the spot, as if in a sense of panic she has no idea what to do next. After a moment, she mumbles something under her bandages, and she certainly doesn't sound very impressed.

"Good luck expecting anything to ever work around this place," Lloyd mutters, turning to me. "I swear, even in the time I've been here, I've seen how it's all falling apart."

"And how long *have* you been here?" the elderly woman asks, not looking up from her cards. "You were here when *we* arrived, that's for sure."

"Well," he replies, "I was here..."

His voice trails off, and after a moment he furrows his brow. He seems lost in thought, as if the question is a difficult one, and then finally he offers an exasperated smile.

"Certainly some days now," he tells me. "To tell the truth, I've been in something of a foggy mood, so I can't quite be more precise. I have a diary upstairs, so I can check and let you know later. But it doesn't matter, not really. I'm just like all the rest of you. Honest!" He turns to the bandaged woman, who's still looking startled in the doorway. "Do *you* remember how many nights I've been here?"

She pauses, before hurriedly shaking her head.

"Like I said, it doesn't matter," he continues, turning to me. "I'm just like everyone else here. And this is your first night, I believe?"

I nod.

"I remember *my* first night," he continues, "or rather, I don't. That's the point." With that, he winks at me.

I wait for him to explain, but suddenly the elderly woman slaps a card triumphantly onto the table.

"Oh, balderdash," the elderly man mutters, setting all his cards down. "I thought I had you there!"

"Sshh!" the girl hisses behind me.

Turning, I see that Matilda has a finger against her lips. She glares at the couple, before looking back down at her book. Now that I'm closer, I can see that she's reading *The Wind in the Willows*. I want to tell her that it's one of my favorite books of all time, but she doesn't seem like she wants to be disturbed, and the last thing *I* want is to be a nuisance. She's gently squeezing a ketchup sachet in her right hand, as if she's using it as a kind of stress reliever.

Feeling very out of place, I turn and look at the coffee machine, which is still rumbling away without actually showing any sign that it might deliver water in the near future.

"I wonder if he's found his latest victim yet," Lloyd says after a moment, looking up toward the top of the far wall, as if he's imagining the snowy street above. "Even if there's no news, he *might* have struck, and the body is simply awaiting discovery. Or perhaps he's merely tracking her through the snow, waiting for his chance. Or I suppose it's possible that he's still on the lookout, still waiting for some timid little mouse to scurry out from one of the city's doors. Matilda, for example."

He pauses, before turning to me.

"If I were him, I'd start near the cathedral," he explains. "Good hunting ground and -"

"For God's sake!" Matilda shrieks suddenly, getting to her feet. "Can't you just shut up?!?"

Hearing a bumping sound over my shoulder, I turn just in time to see that the outburst has startled the bandaged woman, sending her staggering back against the trolley with such force that she almost knocks over the pile of cups.

"You actually *enjoy* this, don't you?" Matilda continues, scowling at Lloyd. "It's like a game to you, or some kind of sport!"

"Steady on," the elderly man mutters. "No need to shout."

Lloyd, meanwhile, seems amused by the outburst.

"I can't sit here and listen to this waffle!" Matilda continues, stepping around the table and storming to the door, swinging her arms while still clutching her book. "The Snowman isn't even a real person! It's just a stupid story!"

"Well there you're dead wrong," Lloyd replies. "Actually, the police -"

"Shut up!" she yells, turning to him.

The landlady staggers back again, evidently startled by the volume.

"Night after night," Matilda continues, her voice rippling with anger and frustration, "I've sat here and listened to you going on and on and on about the Snowman. Don't you have anything else to talk about? How old are you, anyway? Forty? Fifty? And here you are, spending your nights sitting in the basement of a crumby, rundown B&B in Canterbury, boring the rest of us to death with your wittering stories about this Snowman character! Is this how you expected your life to turn out? Do you feel a sense of contentment? Are you looking forward to doing the exact same thing tomorrow night, too? And the night after that? Forever and ever and ever?"

"It's not my fault that he's out there," Lloyd replies forlornly.

"You're pathetic!" Matilda snaps, shaking her head as if she's disgusted by the sight of him. "Utterly, terminally *pathetic*! You actually *want* someone to get murdered tonight, don't you?"

"I never said that!"

"It's obvious! If you wake up tomorrow morning and nobody's been found dead in the snow outside, you'll be disappointed! Admit it!"

He opens his mouth to answer, but suddenly his phone buzzes again.

"Aren't you going to check that?" Matilda asks, shaking with fury now. There might even be a hint of tears in her eyes. "Go on, don't hold back on my account! Maybe you've hit the jackpot and some poor girl is dead right now! Maybe you've got another horrific story to talk about all night!" She checks her watch. "It's almost 3am, he should have struck by now, shouldn't he? Doesn't he realize there are pathetic, bloodless weirdos sitting around waiting for the good news?"

She stares at him for a moment, before stamping her left foot in anger and then storming out of the room. A moment later, I hear her stomping up the stairs, and then I turn to see that the landlady seems frozen in the corner, as if the outburst has left her completely stunned.

"Two of hearts," the elderly man says suddenly.

Turning to him, I'm surprised to see that he and his wife have already shuffled, dealt the cards, and begun to play another round.

I turn to look at Lloyd, and I feel bad as soon as I see his hurt expression.

"I was only trying to keep the conversation going," he mutters finally. "You know, to jolly things along a little. I didn't mean to cause offense."

"She's highly-strung, that one," the elderly woman replies, not taking her eyes off her cards. "It's all the reading that does it. She fills her head with nonsense, and then she doesn't understand how the *real* world works. I tried to get her to play with us, but she thinks she's above it all. She just sits behind us, night after night, with her nose stuck in that folly of a book. God knows what she expects." She sniffs haughtily, making no effort to hide her disdain. "Won't get her anywhere, not in the long-run. She's just lost in her own world, with its own rules and -"

Before she can finish, the coffee machine suddenly lets out a very loud grinding sound, almost as if it's starting to eat itself. The whole thing shudders and shakes on the counter, getting louder and louder, until it falls silent just as suddenly as it started up. I stare at it, and a moment later a dribble of steaming hot water starts running down from the spout and into my cup.

"See?" Lloyd says finally. "Told you it'd get going eventually. It just takes a little time, that's all."

Suddenly the landlady mutters something, but her panicked voice is muffled by the bandages. She hurries past the machine and out the door, and then I hear her hurrying up the stairs.

"World of her own, that one," Lloyd continues, nudging my arm. "Nice enough, but God alone knows what goes through her head."

"Do you know what happened to her face?" I ask. "Why does she wear those bandages?"

"I'm not entirely sure," he replies, "although I *did* spot a big tube of lotion in her office once. Something to do with treating bites or stings, or inflammation of some kind. I don't entirely recall now." He pauses. "It's a strange old set-up, to be sure. In fact, I'm not even certain that..."

His voice trails off for a moment, as if he's lost in thought.

"Well, I must have," he adds finally, forcing a smile. "Mustn't I?"

"But she's alright?" I continue. "I mean..."

I *want* to ask if she's sane, or at least trustworthy, but I'm not quite sure how to phrase the question without sounding mean.

"Best not to worry too much about these things," Lloyd says after a moment. "Take a leaf out of my book. I could be horribly offended by everything that Matilda said just now, but I just led it slide off like water from a duck's back. Other people can be strange, but you have to stay true to yourself at all times. That's the key to a happy life, and I should know. I honestly believe that I'm the happiest man I've ever met!"

He certainly seems to have recovered from his shock at Matilda's tirade, and I suppose there's something to be said for resilience. If somebody had yelled at *me* with such vehemence, I'd have collapsed into myself and carried the criticism around for the rest of my life, whereas Lloyd has already brushed the whole thing off. I actually envy him. Then again, I guess he might be holding onto her words deep down, even if he's not showing any signs on the surface.

"Your tea will be ready," he tells me.

For a moment, I'm honestly not sure what he means, but then I remember and look toward the machine. Sure enough, a steaming cup of tea is waiting beneath the spout.

"You really should join us for a game," he continues. "There's no pressure, obviously, but do you honestly think you'll be able to sleep tonight? It's already three."

"I should probably try," I reply, heading back

over to the machine and carefully taking the cup without burning myself. Suddenly the thought of going to bed is pretty appealing. "Thanks all the same."

"Tomorrow night, then?"

"I'm leaving in the morning."

"Well that's a darned pity," he continues, leaning back in his chair. "We could use a shake-up around here. Lately it feels like it's just the same people, bumbling about night after night. As you can no doubt tell, we've begun to rather get on one another's nerves."

"I'm sure someone else will be along soon," I tell him. "Someone new."

He turns to the elderly couple. "Who was the last new arrival?" he asks them.

The woman shrugs, and a moment later the man does the same.

"It's so long now," Lloyd continues, seemingly drifting into his own thoughts, "that I'm not sure I remember."

"How long are *you* staying for?" I ask.

He stares into space for a few seconds, before turning to me. "Well that's a complicated matter. I'm afraid I'm not entirely..."

Again, his voice trails off.

"Well I'm sure everything will be fine," I continue. "And now I really have to get to bed, but maybe I'll see you at breakfast before I leave."

I wait for one of them to say something, but the old man and woman are focusing on their game while Lloyd seems suddenly lost in his own mind. I mutter something about hoping they have a fun night, and then I head out of the room. My tea is still too hot to sip, so I blow on it a little as I get to the next floor. Just as I'm about to go up the next flight of stairs, however, I feel a sudden cold gust of wind blowing against my left side. Turning, I see to my surprise that the B&B's front door has been left wide open, allowing snow from the storm to drift through and start settling on the mat.

I look around, but there's no sign of anyone. Wandering over to the office door, I look through, but again there's no-one around at all. The hallway is getting much colder now, so I make my way to the front door, ready to swing it shut. Just as I'm about to do so, however, I spot a set of footprints in the snow outside, and a moment later I realize there are prints on the steps too. More snow is already falling and filling the prints, but it's quite clear that somebody left the building at some point during the past few minutes.

Leaning out, I look both ways along the deserted street. Snow covers the ground, while more falls from the pitch-black sky, and the only sound is the rustle of snow upon snow.

"Hello?" I call out, immediately hearing my own voice echoing back at me.

I look down at the prints again, but it's not really possible to tell anything about the person who went out. Still, I can't -

Suddenly there's a loud ringing sound from one of the B&B's nearby rooms. I turn and look back along the corridor, and I realize that the phone is ringing in the office. A moment later, I hear footsteps coming up from the basement, and Lloyd appears at the corridor's far

57

end.

"I think somebody went outside," I tell him.

"Is nobody else here to answer that?" he asks.

I shake my head.

Muttering something under his breath, he heads to the office door and then leans through, taking the phone off the hook and holding it to his ear.

"Hello," he says calmly, checking his watch. "You've reached the -"

He stops suddenly, furrowing his brow as he listens to whoever's on the other end of the line.

"Who is it?" I ask, heading over to join him.

He sighs.

"Who is it?" I ask again. A moment later I hear a faint bumping sound coming from the stairs, but there's no sign of anyone when I look over.

Lloyd holds the phone up as I turn back to him, and now I can hear the voice.

"And I'm still alive," Matilda says matter-of-factly, sounding rather pleased with herself. "I haven't been knifed or strangled yet, so I guess you were wrong about that Snowman character after all, weren't you?"

"Is she serious?" I ask, shocked by her apparent stupidity. "Did she really go out there in this weather?"

"So there's nobody here outside the public library," she continues. "Now I think I'll go on a little tour and call you from every phone box I can find. The next one's in the cathedral precinct, isn't it? I'll give you a ring in five, Lloyd. Unless the nasty Snowman gets me first!"

She laughs as she hangs up.

"She's serious," I stammer, watching as he puts the phone back on the hook. "What the hell is she trying to prove?"

"That I'm an old fool," he mutters.

"You're not the only person who's talked about this Snowman guy," I tell him.

"I might have exaggerated a little," he continues, "but *only* a little. There's definitely a nasty chap who seems to commit one murder in the city every time there's snow."

He steps past me and looks out at the snow-covered street.

"I do wish she'd been a little more sensible," he mutters. "This is how bad situations start. It's certainly not the kind of night for a young lady to be out alone."

Heading over to join him, I peer out at the street. The city is so quiet, it's hard to believe that anything bad could happen, but at the same time I don't like the idea of Matilda being out there by herself. It's still hard to believe that she'd be so stupid, although clearly she's been getting wound up by Lloyd for quite some time now, and I guess I understand why she'd want to make some big demonstration to prove him wrong. And she'll probably be fine. I mean, the odds of this Snowman guy actually being out there are low, and the odds of him bumping into her are even lower.

"What's that?" I ask, spotting a faint light in the distance, moving slowly along the next street.

"One of those busybodies, I imagine," he replies.

"Who?"

"A kind of night-watch group who..." His voice

trails off for a moment, as the light disappears from view. "I didn't know they were still around," he continues. "I thought they'd disbanded a long time ago. They're just a group of old codgers who try to make themselves feel better by patrolling the streets on snowy nights. They think they can make a difference, but they can't. They've never stopped a murder yet, and they certainly won't be any use to poor Matilda."

"I wouldn't worry too much," I say finally, turning to him. "I'm sure she'll be -"

Suddenly the phone rings again.

"No prizes for guessing who *that* is," Lloyd says with a sigh, turning and heading back to the office so he can answer. "Hello, Matilda," he continues as he picks up the phone. "Listen, you've proved your point and -"

"I still haven't been murdered," she replies, interrupting him as he turns the phone so I can hear it too. "Oh, the cathedral is so pretty in all this snow. I wish you could see it, but I suppose you're far too much of a scaredy-cat. One good thing about all this nonsense is that I've got the entire city to myself. I can dance and sing and do whatever I want out here, and nobody is going to stop me."

"Maybe you should come back," I tell her, hoping against hope that she'll listen. "Aren't you cold?"

"I'm not coming back 'til I've called from every phone box in the city," she says firmly. "You haven't sat there for night after night, listening to Lloyd's constant rambling conversation about the Snowman. I have! God, he's so -"

Suddenly she gasps.

Lloyd and I wait, but now she's fallen silent.

"Matilda?" I say cautiously. "Are you still there?"

Again, we wait.

Finally there's a faint bumping sound on the other end of the line.

"Matilda?" I say again. "Are you -"

"It's nothing," she mutters, sounding a little stressed. "I just... I thought I heard..."

Her voice trails off for a moment.

"It's nothing," she adds, adding a laugh that seems forced. "I'm just all alone here in the precinct outside the cathedral, and there's no-one else around. You're just jealous, that's all. At least I'm -"

And then she gasps again.

Lloyd and I wait.

"Matilda?" I ask finally. "What's going on?"

"Nothing," she stammers, but now she sounds much less sure of herself. "I just... It's nothing. For a moment there, I just thought I heard -"

Suddenly there's a bumping sound, followed by a brief rattle, and then what seems to be something crashing through the snow. My heart is pounding as I listen, but finally the sound fades.

"Matilda?" I ask. "Are you there?"

"Matilda?" Lloyd adds. "Come on, young lady, this isn't the right time to be playing pranks!"

The line is still open, and I think I can hear the rustle of more falling snow on the other end, but there's no longer any hint of Matilda.

"She's just trying to scare us, right?" I say

finally, turning to Lloyd. "This has to be her idea of a joke!"

I wait for him to say something, but instead we simply stand in silence for a moment, waiting for some sign that Matilda is okay. As the seconds tick past, however, I can't shake the feeling that maybe this isn't a joke at all, that maybe something really *has* happened to her.

"Don't panic just yet," Lloyd says cautiously, even though I can see the fear in his eyes. "I'm sure she's alright. I mean, that's what *you* said a moment ago, so..."

I want to tell him that she *will* be alright, but deep down I'm starting to worry. I pause for a moment, before turning and heading to the stairs.

"Where are you going?" he asks.

"Where do you think?" I hurry to my room and grab my jacket, before running back down and finding that Lloyd is standing at the open front door. "I'm going outside to find her."

"You can't be serious!"

"Call the police," I continue, hurrying down the steps, "and tell them -"

Suddenly my right foot slips on the ice. I reach out and grab the railing, managing just in time to keep from tumbling down, although in the process I feel a sharp pain in my arm as I pull on the muscle. I tread more carefully until I'm down in the snow, and then I look back up at Lloyd.

"Are you coming with me?" I ask breathlessly.

He hesitates for a moment. "It's not safe," he stammers finally. "I mean... We should stay here."

"There's no time!" I tell him. "Go to the -"

Before I can finish, I spot a figure in the distance, rushing through the snow. I squint, struggling to make the figure out properly, but all I can really tell is that it's a woman and she's not carrying a light. She has a similar dress to Matilda, and as she comes closer I'm convinced it's her. At first I breathe a sigh of relief, figuring she's coming back to the B&B, but after a moment I realize she seems to be panicking. Just as I'm about to call out to her, she takes a sudden turn, darting down a side-street and disappearing from view.

"What the heck?" I whisper, turning to Lloyd. "There's a turning just by the bank on the corner. Where does it lead?"

He furrows his brow. "That's just the alley that runs behind these buildings. It comes out around the corner, but it only goes past the rear of the B&B."

"What's she doing going down there?" I ask. "Is she -"

Suddenly I hear a scream in the distance. Muffled and faint, but definitely a scream.

I turn to Lloyd.

"I'm sure it was nothing," he replies, but I can see the fear in his eyes. "I was joking earlier, obviously. The odds of her running into the Snowman are so small... Please, you mustn't put yourself at risk for such an irritating young lady."

"I'm going to check the alley," I stammer, hurrying past him and heading through to the rear of the building. "Lloyd, call the police!"

"But -"

"Call them!"

It takes a moment, but finally I find the back door and I spill out into the pitch-black, snow-covered alley just in time to hear another scream. And this time, it's definitely Matilda.

CHAPTER FOUR

"WHERE ARE YOU?" I yell, wading through the snow, almost stumbling a couple of times. "Matilda! Can -"

Suddenly I bump against something buried in the snow. Falling forward, I barely have time to raise my hands before I slam into the wall. I feel a sharp pain in my ankle but I keep pushing on, desperately trying to get further along the alley. It'd help if I could see anything, but the moon has slipped behind a thick bank of clouds.

"Matilda!" I shout. "Say something!"

Stopping, I look back the way I just came, but there's no sign of anyone. Lloyd had better be on the phone to the police right now, but I don't have time to go and check. I look ahead again, hoping against hope that I'll spot some sign of Matilda in the snow. Instead, however, the moon reappears and I see something dark sprinkled against the white just a few feet away. I wade over to take a closer look.

Blood.

"Oh no," I whisper, "please, no..."

The blood is in two big dollops and doesn't look to be sinking deep into the snow. My mind is racing and I'm convinced that something really bad must be happening out here, even though there's no sign of an attack. Stepping back, I look both ways, and finally I realize that I'm completely defenseless. I've handled myself in tough situations before, but never anything quite like this, and I think maybe I should've at least grabbed a knife from the kitchen before I came out here.

I take another step back, as snow is blown against my face.

Suddenly I hear a voice giggling nearby.

Startled, I look toward the shadows. I step back again as soon as I spot movement, but the giggling is continuing and it's sounding more and more like a girl. Finally, I'm shocked to see Matilda emerging into a patch of snowy moonlight, and she quickly tosses something small down onto the snow next to me. When I pick it up, I find myself holding a twisted, squeezed-out ketchup sachet.

"Your face!" Matilda says, still laughing. "Priceless! Isn't Lloyd with you? He's the one I *really* wanted to freak out. Can you go get him and bring him out here, so I can scare him? Please?"

"You staged this?" I ask, looking down at the dollops of ketchup that I'd somehow, unbelievably, mistaken for blood. "But I heard you scream..."

"You mean like this?"

Suddenly another shrill scream fills the air. I put my hands over my ears until it stops.

"I'm so sick of the way everyone talks about that goddamn Snowman," she continues with a grin. "You understand, don't you? Lloyd and the others skulk about in the B&B night after night, going on and on about this terrifying killer who only strikes when there's snow. I swear, even if there really *is* a killer on the loose, I'd rather meet *him* on a dark night instead of listening to one more of Lloyd's long, rambling soliloquies about how we all have to be *so* careful. If he had his way, none of us would ever leave that goddamn basement again."

"You *staged* this?" I ask again, still struggling to believe that she'd be so completely stupid. "For a joke? You really -"

Suddenly she screams again.

"Stop that!" I hiss, putting my hands back over my ears.

"I just did it to prove a point," she replies, wading past me as she heads toward the B&B's back door. "I've listened to Lloyd night after night after night, since..."

She stops, and when she turns to me I realize that there's a hint of confusion in her eyes.

"Well, since as long as I can remember," she adds, "which is..."

She pauses, her face a picture of doubt, before finally she forces a smile.

"Oh, I don't know. Sometimes I feel like it's been forever since I arrived in this miserable city. I'm sure keen to get moving, though. I can't wait to leave."

"And when *are* you leaving?" I ask.

"Soon."

"When?"

She shrugs. "Soon. I don't remember exactly, I'll have to go to the office some time and check. It can be hard to keep track of things like that."

She takes a step back, while keeping her eyes fixed on me.

"Oh God," she continues. "You're not like Lloyd, are you?"

"Like Lloyd?"

"Don't you have a sense of humor? Can't you see the funny side?"

"I can -"

She screams yet again.

"Stop!" I shout, shuddering at the shrillness of her voice.

She starts laughing. "I've got a good scream, huh?" she says after a moment. "It's one of my best features."

"I thought you'd been attacked," I tell her, feeling my fear slowly starting to become anger. "Lloyd's probably on the phone to the police right now. We both thought you were in trouble. I thought I saw blood on the snow and -"

"That was ketchup, silly!"

"I know it was ketchup *now*!" I shout, before realizing that there's no point letting myself get too worked-up. Matilda's clearly nothing more than a dumb, immature kid with no real understanding of the world, and I have neither the time nor the inclination to even *try* setting her straight.

"It's cold out here," she says after a moment,

turning and forcing her way through the snow until she reaches the back door. "I'm going inside to warm myself up. Are you coming?"

"In a minute," I stammer, wanting to let her get ahead of me so I don't have to listen to her infuriating, rambling voice for even a moment longer. Besides, she'll probably want to demonstrate her scream again. "I just need to do something out here first."

"Suit yourself."

With that, she disappears inside, leaving me standing all alone in the snow. I know I shouldn't stay out here, but I honestly can't stand the thought of being anywhere near that annoying girl right now. I figure I'll just wait a minute or two and then I'll go straight up to my room, and hopefully I won't see her again, not even tomorrow morning at breakfast. I'm starting to think that this B&B is a little too crazy for my liking, and that I'd be better off getting out of here as soon as I can. Part of me thinks that getting out of here right now would preserve my sanity, but part of me doesn't like the idea of sleeping on a bench at the station during a snowstorm. Besides, I've always run from problems in the past. It'd be good for me to stick it out, and it's not like things can get any weirder. I'll just go to my room, shut the door, and sleep until morning.

Once I've left enough time for Matilda to be out of the way, I start wading through the snow, making slow progress as I head toward the back door. Snow is soaking through my trousers now and my legs are aching, and all I can think about is the soft, warm bed that's waiting for me upstairs. If I just -

Suddenly a figure slams into me from behind, knocking me off my feet and landing right on top of me as I hit the ground.

I try to cry out, but my voice is muffled, and I try to break free only to find that I'm being held far too tight. Still desperately wriggling, I can feel hot breath on the side of my neck. I try again to scream, but the hand pushes through the snow and covers my mouth again, and then my body is twisted around. I feel someone clambering on top of me, kneeling on my chest and forcing me deeper into the snow. The pressure is so immense, I can barely breathe at all.

My eyes are wide with terror, but all I can see is the faintest silhouette above me, barely visible against the dark night sky.

I try again to get my hands free, but they're being held far too tight. I can hear my attacker grunting, as if he's struggling to hold me down, but he's clearly far too strong. Tilting my head back, I let out a muffled cry, desperately trying to open my mouth and scream despite the hand that's clamped tight against my face. I can see the rear of the B&B building, and there are lights in some of the windows, but I just can't quite manage to shout for help. Besides, before I can cry out, I need to get some air into my lungs.

I struggle again, straining every muscle in my body, but nothing seems to work as I try to wriggle free. No matter how hard I try to cry out for help, the hand over my mouth muffles my screams so that they're nothing more than a perpetual, agonized hum. Tears are streaming down my face, and suddenly it occurs to me that maybe the only way out of here is to somehow turn and try burrowing down into the snow. As soon as I try, however, my left shoulder is slammed back down with such force that I involuntarily let out another pained gurgle. Tilting my head back, I look toward the B&B, desperately hoping that someone is going to come and save me from this brutal, grunting monster.

And that's when I see her.

The bandaged landlady is at one of the brightly-lit upper windows, staring straight down at me. I swear I can even see her eyes glinting in the snow-light, watching me as I continue to struggle. She must be able to see what's happening, but she's not lifting a finger to help. It's almost as if she just wants to watch as this monster has his way with me.

I try again to cry out, but I feel as if there's not an ounce of air in my lungs. I know I have to stay strong, and my mind is racing as I try to think of a way out of this, but my body seems to be becoming a terrified, shaking mess.

"Help me!" I try to gasp, weeping as the hand clamps even tighter over my mouth. "Somebody help me..."

I feel fingers pressing against my belly.

My eyes are fixed on the bandaged woman as she continues to watch me. No matter how hard I try to fight back, this monster has me pinned down. Is the woman simply going to watch while I'm killed? Is she in on it all?

If this is the end, it means I never got to atone for what I did. I would've gone home eventually, I swear, and faced the punishment for what I did. I would have tried to -

Suddenly the monster pulls back, letting go of my mouth and hauling itself aside through the snow. Startled, I sit up, just in time to see the figure wading frantically through the snow as it rushes away from me. For a fraction of a second, I'm convinced that this is only a temporary reprieve, but soon the figure has disappeared into the darkness entirely. Although I feel no pain in my belly, I still reach down with shaking hands and fumble beneath my shirt, terrified in case I find wounds and injuries that have cut deep. Maybe I just haven't felt them yet.

There's nothing.

He didn't cut me.

I scramble to my feet and clamber, sobbing and wailing, through the snow. I look up at the B&B's window and see that the bandaged woman is still there, still watching me impassively, and then I force my way to the back door. Finally, exhausted and aching, I drop down onto the carpet before hauling myself back up and pushing the door shut. Quickly finding the bolt, I slide it across and then slump back against the wall, desperately trying to get my breath back.

For the next few minutes, I search frantically for any cuts or stab-wounds on my body, but there really *is* nothing at all. I was down for the count in the snow, the monster could have done anything he wanted to me, yet apart from a twisted ankle I'm completely fine. I can only assume that something must have scared him off. Maybe he saw the woman in the window, although it's hard to believe she was enough to make him run.

She was just watching.

Waiting.

Almost as if she *wanted* to see something awful happen to me.

Forcing myself up, I lean against the wall for a moment before stumbling along the corridor. My clothes are soaking wet, with clumps of snow frozen stiff to the fabric. My right ankle is killing me, but I think pure adrenaline might be masking the worst of the pain so I keep going and finally I start hobbling up the stairs. When I reach the bend, I stumble again and reach out, supporting myself against the large plant pot. As I do so, my right hand brushes against one of the large, juicy leaves, and I feel an instant scratch of irritation. Letting out a gasp, I pull my hand away and see that there's already a faint red rash. Whatever this damn plant is made of, it's clearly not good for human skin, but fortunately that won't matter for long.

I'm getting the hell out of this B&B.

My legs are aching so much from all the snow, and it takes another couple of minutes before I reach the landing. Limping over to the door to room four, I fumble for the key and finally get inside. I don't know where I'm going to go once I leave this place, but staying here is definitely not an option. I'll sleep at the station, and then I'll get a train to London, or I'll go home. There'll be time to make a final decision later. Grabbing my suitcase, I haul it off the bed and drag it back out onto the landing.

I glance at the nearby window. I'm pretty sure this is where the bandaged woman was standing a few minutes ago, while she calmly watched me getting attacked in the alley, but she's gone now. Then again, she might have been in one of the rooms. It's hard to tell for sure.

"Bitch!" I mutter under my breath. "Goddamn -"

Spotting movement nearby, I turn and look at the next set of stairs. Somebody is creeping down, not making any noise at all, and a moment later the timid, long-haired woman comes into view once more. She freezes as soon as she sees me, and then she starts backing away, heading up the stairs again.

"It's okay," I tell her. "I'm not -"

I sigh as she withdraws once more into the shadows.

"I'm not going to bite," I add, although I guess it's too late. Whatever's up with her, she seems perpetually terrified.

Turning, I look back at the spot where the bandaged woman stood earlier when she was watching me.

"Thanks for nothing," I mutter darkly, looking around at the doors for a moment before turning and starting the slow, painful job of lugging my suitcase downstairs. "God forbid that you'd actually *help* someone who's being attacked by a monster!"

Each step is difficult, and I soon have to stop to get my breath back.

I can see the stupid plant ahead, sitting in its stupid pot with its stupid fronds reaching over the edges. My hand is really itching now, but I figure the irritation will heal soon enough. Besides, that's the least of my problems.

"Okay," I whisper under my breath, bracing myself to drag the suitcase down a few more steps. "Time to -"

Before I can get another word out, my damaged ankle buckles beneath me. I try to steady myself but I'm too late and I tumble down, landing against the pot with enough force to push my face straight into the heart of the evil plant. I wince as I pull back, but one of the fronds cut my cheek and I can already feel a stinging sensation on my cheek and forehead.

"Great!" I hiss, hauling myself up and grabbing the suitcase. "This is just the house that keeps on giving!"

I pull on the suitcase, only to find that it's caught on one of the steps. I pull again, and this time it comes loose, almost sending me thudding down against the plant yet again. Fortunately I manage to hold myself up this time, although my face is really starting to burn now.

Determined to get out of here, I push through the pain and drag my suitcase all the way to the hall. I can't hear any voices talking in the breakfast room below, so hopefully everyone has finally gone to bed. I make my way straight to the door that leads into the office. There's no sign of the bandaged landlady, although I'm not even sure what I'd say if I found her. Honestly, I think I'd just thank her for the complete lack of help earlier. Clearly she's running some kind of insane set-up here, but it's none of my business and I just want to get out of the damn place.

Leaning through the doorway, I hang the key to room four on the hook. Just as I'm about to turn and leave, however, I spot a large bottle of anti-irritation lotion on the table.

I glance up the stairs, before figuring that the least I'm owed is a little relief from the increasing pain caused by that goddamn plant.

I haul my suitcase into the room and head to the table. Grabbing the bottle of lotion, I turn it around and take a look at the label. Sure enough, it's specifically designed to deal with pain and lesions caused by certain types of plant. I guess the landlady has had a few run-ins with the damn thing already, so I open the bottle and squeeze some of the thick white lotion onto my irritated hand. Almost immediately, I feel the pain starting to subside.

I wait a moment, just to make sure that there are no side-effects, and then I squeeze out more lotion, quickly slathering it all over my face. The relief is instant, and I add a second layer and then a third.

Glancing across the room, I spot a phone in the corner.

I pause for a moment, before limping over and picking up the receiver. For a few seconds I actually consider calling the police, but I'm not entirely sure what I'd say. This B&B is certainly weird, but it's not like anyone has done anything illegal, and my story of finding a dead man in the bathtub would probably get laughed out of consideration. I can't even begin to separate the genuine weirdness from the parts that were all in my head. Setting the receiver back down, I suddenly realize that my hand and face are itching again, as if the lotion is starting to wear off. I head back to the table and read the rest of the label, only to find that the damn thing only works if it's used in conjunction with aloe-treated bandaged.

Sure enough, there's a huge bundle of bandages on the table in the corner.

I want to get out of here, but my snow-soaked clothes are freezing against my skin and I'm starting to shiver. Sleeping on a bench might be fatal in this weather. There's a fireplace on the far side of the room, so I limp over and take a closer look. Spotting a box of matches, I take one out and use it to try setting light to the wood, so I can get a little heat. The wood seems burned already, and charred, so I set the matches aside and grab the iron poker that's resting against the wall. I use it to push the wood around, before realizing that this is hopeless. I'm never going to get a fire spotted.

Turning, I spot an electric heater nearby. My ankle is throbbing, so I lean on the metal poker, using it as a walking stick as I start hobbling across the room.

Suddenly the poker's tapered tip breaks through a gap between the floorboards, sliding down to the hilt. I fall, landing on my hands and knees, still holding the handle of the poker.

"Great!" I hiss, wiggling the handle for a moment, trying to pull it out. Finally, after a couple of tries, I manage to start sliding the iron poker up, pulling it from the hole in the floor. Figuring that there's no point relying on it again, I toss it away and then get to my feet, preferring to hobble unaided to the electric heater.

I swing the door shut and then I start peeling out of my stiff, partially-frozen clothes. The process takes several minutes, but finally I'm left in nothing but my semi-dry underwear, and I carefully hang my clothes on the backs of several chairs. They should be at least partly dry in just a few minutes, and I can use that time to deal with my increasingly painful face.

I grab the bandages and tear away a long strip, which I wrap haphazardly across my forehead. I hold it in place for a few seconds, before breathing a sigh of relief as I feel the pain fading away. I know this entire situation is ridiculous, but I can't leave while my face is so painful, so I grab more strips of bandage and start wrapping them all over the affected parts of my face, while muttering to myself about all the terrible things that have happened to me during this awful night.

And then, of all the things that could happen next, somebody actually knocks on the front door.

"Oh, go away," I mutter, panicking in case the knock brings the landlady back down, or encourages Lloyd and the others to come up. The last thing I need is to be interrupted, so I focus on wrapping more and more bandages around my head.

Suddenly I hear another knock.

"Shut up!" I hiss. "Quiet! You'll wake them!"

Figuring that I just have to tell the visitor to go away, I look around for my jacket before realizing that I must have left it in my room. The landlady's gown is hanging from a hook, however, so I grab *that* and slip into it before shuffling out into the hallway. I swear, even if it's the goddamn Snowman himself waiting outside, I'm just gonna tell him to get lost. This entire absurd situation has to end, and I want to get away without any more of the B&B's ridiculous inhabitants bothering me. I am so completely done with all the insanity tonight.

Still muttering dark thoughts under my breath, I pull the door open and see a figure down in the snow, dragging a suitcase away.

I freeze.

The figure stops and turns to look at me.

I stare at her, too shocked to say a word, convinced that there has to be some kind of terrible mistake here.

It's me.

The person who just knocked on the door, the person down there in the snow, the person who's now staring up at me as I stand here with a fully bandaged head...

It's me.

I mean, she's me.

I mean...

..what?

CHAPTER FIVE

"SORRY," SHE SAYS, LETTING go of her suitcase's handle, "is this -"

She stops suddenly as the sign creaks above us, blown by the increasingly rough and snowy gale.

"Do you have any rooms available?" she continues. "I know it's late. I tried calling from the phone-box at the station, but no-one answered. All the other B&B numbers I tried were full, so I figured..."

I wait, but her voice has trailed off.

Staring at her, I try to figure out what's happening here. She *looks* like me, she's wearing *my* clothes, she even appears to have my suitcase, but clearly she can't actually *be* me. This has to be the latest sick, disturbed joke that the people of this B&B are playing on me, although I can't even begin to imagine how they could do such a thing. Either that, or I've finally lost my mind. The person I'm staring at simply *can't* be me.

I must be having some kind of psychotic episode.

Or a stroke.

She's not real. This is all in my head, and the more I look at her, the more I feel as if I might faint.

Feeling a sudden rush of panic in my chest, I swing the door shut with enough force to leave it rattling in the frame. I take a deep breath, silently counting to three, and then I pull it open again.

She's still there.

I stare at her, waiting to figure out what's going on.

She stares back at me, as if she expects me to say something.

"I don't want to cause any trouble," she says finally, looking over at the window before turning back to me. "I really just wanted to see if you had any rooms available for the night. I'm just kinda passing through, that's all. But if you don't have any vacancies, then..."

Is that what I said earlier? Like, is that it, word for word? I'm not certain, even though it was only a few hours ago, but it definitely *sounds* like she's saying what I said. Snow is still falling, perhaps thicker and faster than ever, but the girl with my face is still just staring at me as if she thinks I'll suddenly say something that explains the entire mess.

"Okay, then," she says with a faint, nervous smile. "Sorry to disturb you. I'll try somewhere else."

I watch as she turns and starts dragging her suitcase away. She looks pathetic, struggling through the snow like that. In fact, she looks like she might collapse at any moment. I definitely didn't look *that* pathetic earlier.

"Wait!" I stammer, feeling as if I desperately need her to stay until I figure this out. At the same time, I realize my throat is extremely dry, which I guess was caused by the plant fronds when they brushed against my lips. My voice sounds harsh and coarse, barely recognizable.

She stops and looks at me.

"Come in," I continue, not really knowing what else to do. It's cold out here, and the landlady's gown is way too thin to keep me warm, so I gesture for the girl to come inside and then I step back into the darkness and relative warmth of the hallway.

What the hell am I doing?

Why am I inviting her in?

This is madness. I'm *encouraging* madness. Then again, I need to face whatever's going on here.

I take a couple more steps back, and after a moment I hear the girl trampling through the snow. She starts hauling her suitcase up the steps, and it's clear that she's struggling slightly, but finally she drags it all the way to the top and then she stops for a few seconds, framed in the doorway.

Worried that she might get too close, I turn and shuffle back into the office, where my clothes are still drying on the chairs near the electric heater. Stepping over, I reach out and check my shirt, although I find that it's still pretty wet, which means I guess I should keep the gown on for a while. I don't know whether the landlady is going to come through at any moment, but at least this time I'll know where to start when it comes to all my questions. And I sure have a *lot* of questions of questions for that woman.

Hurrying over to the desk, I pull the first drawer open and take a look inside. A moment later, however, I hear a shuffling sound nearby, and I turn to see that the girl is watching me from the corridor.

"Who are you?" I whisper quietly, almost too shocked to actually get any words out at all.

Figuring that I can go through the desk later, I make my way cautiously back toward the door. This girl certainly looks a lot like me, but my eyesight has never been the best in the world and I figure that maybe the similarity isn't quite as strong as I'd first thought. As soon as I get closer, however, I realize that she seems to be an exact copy of me, down to every last detail, which is both creepy and fascinating at the same time. Even her clothes look the same as the clothes that I have hanging over the chairs right now.

I tilt my head slightly.

She's my exact double.

"So how much is it?" she asks, looking at the key on the hook. "A room, I mean. I don't want to put you out, but I'm kinda in a bind. I didn't expect to be coming here today, and then I didn't have time to call ahead, and I don't have a phone with me. It's kind of a funny story how I ended up here, I actually -"

She stops suddenly, and after a moment she puts her right hand in her pocket. She's fumbling with something in there, and I quickly remember how I counted out some notes earlier when I was in her position. The only possible explanation is that she must have watched video footage of my arrival earlier tonight, and now she's doing her very best to copy my every move. I can't even begin to imagine why anyone would want to go to so much trouble just to trick me, but there are no other possible explanations. I'm impressed by her attention to detail.

Finally she slips some notes from her pocket.

"I'll be paying cash," she explains. "You *are* the owner, right? I just want a room, somewhere to sleep. I'm not fussy, but..."

Again, her voice trails off.

I should make her leave. Or rather, I should let her stay and *I* should leave. Whatever's going on here, I should just get as far away as possible from this B&B. At the same time, however, I want to know what she really is, and where she came from, and why she's tormenting me. And I *need* to know if this is really happening, or if it's all in my head.

"Okay, then," she says suddenly, "maybe I really *should* get going. I'm sure I can find another B&B, and if not I can always try to get the last train to London, or I can sleep at the station and leave in the morning. I'll just be on my way and leave you in peace."

Turning, she makes her way back toward the door.

"No!" I call out. "Wait!"

She glances back at me.

For a moment, I'm not entirely sure what to do, but suddenly I spot the wooden counter propped up next to the door and I swing it down into place. There are some forms nearby, so I take one and start writing a few details, while mumbling my name to myself. After a moment, however, I realize that it's absurd to put all this down on the form, so I push the piece of paper aside.

My heart is pounding.

What if this is a dream?

Or what if I'm completely insane?

Yeah, that could be it. Maybe I cracked. Maybe after everything I've been through over the past few days, my brain just popped and send me completely around the bend. It's not like I haven't been worrying about something like that happening. In fact, I've spent a lot of time reading up on mental illness and schizophrenia, hoping that I'll be able to spot the warning signs, but I guess it's possible that the whole thing simply snuck up on me. I'm probably standing here completely alone right now, rambling on to myself, imagining this copy of me and slipping deeper and deeper into some form of psychosis.

Either that, or there really *is* a copy of me here at the B&B. But why would that happen? Who'd be behind it all? Still, I'm starting to think that maybe she's not an *exact* copy. In fact, the more I watch her, the more I realize that she seems very weak, almost timid, like a scared little country mouse. I mean, I *can* be timid sometimes, but not like this.

She's actually kinda annoying.

"Are you okay?" she asks, as if to underline that point. "Is this a bad time? I just -"

"Room four," I reply, to interrupt her and cut off her slightly whiny voice. My voice is never, *ever* that whiny and nasal. In fact, her voice is all the proof I need that she's a fake. There's no way I sound like her, not in real life. The cracks in her mimicry are starting to show.

I take the key to room four from the hook. It's the only one that's free, so I guess I have to give it to her, at least while I figure this mess out. "I suppose. Yeah. I guess you should take room four. It's the only one that's... It's the only one that's free."

"And how much is that?"

Is this another part of the trap?

"What?" I stammer.

"How much is a room for the night?"

"Oh." She's a very good actress. Whoever she is and whatever she's doing, and whyever she's doing it, she's doing a great job of imitating me. She just needs to drop the whiny tone a few notches and try not to look so pathetic. If it wasn't for the nasal voice, I might actually be convinced. "The usual," I continue, trying to remember from earlier. "What was it? Forty-five? Sure. Forty-five pounds."

"That seems kinda cheap."

I shrug, which causes the bandages to rustle.

"Okay." She counts some notes from her handful and sets them on the counter. She seems so hesitant and nervous, I want to slap her. This is another crack in her facade, the unrealistic part of her mimicry. She's like a meek, pathetic version of me. "And that includes breakfast?" she asks after a moment.

"I suppose it does, yeah," I tell her. "Sure."

"My name's Bobbie," she replies. "Roberta, actually, but people call me Bobbie. Don't you need to take my details?"

"Details?"

"So I can stay the night?"

I swallow hard. She's really taking this thing all the way, although I think I can see a hint of fear in her eyes, like maybe she's worried I'll call her out. I guess I should still play along until I've got the situation figured out.

"Roberta Simmons," she adds, taking a provisional license from her wallet.

Her hand is trembling slightly. She's trying to hide it, but she can't. I'm onto her.

I immediately grab the license and tilt it toward the light. I've got to admit, the facsimile is impressive. My license is somewhere in one of my pockets, in the clothes that are drying on the chair, but I have no doubt that this copy is very, very close to the real thing. When I tilt it a little further, I see that it even has the hologram printing, which means it's not just a cheap knock-off. Whoever this girl is, she clearly has access to people who know what they're doing, and I can't help eyeing her suspiciously between the slits in my bandages.

This is a test.

She's staring at me gormlessly, looking totally lost, but she's definitely testing me. Waiting for my reaction. The last thing I want to do is panic, so I guess I just have to play things cool.

And I *can* be cool.

"Okay," I say, forcing a relaxed smile that she probably can't see because of the bandages. I set the license down. "Fine. Okay. I get it."

"Sorry?"

I watch as she takes the license.

"Okay," I continue, making sure to put her at ease and demonstrate that I'm not freaked out. "Sure."

She furrows her brow. She's good at this.

"Sure what?" she asks.

"Sure... Sure you can have the room. Why not, right?"

"Thank you," she says meekly. Again, just seems very timid and scared, and I'm starting to find her quite irritating.

Figuring I need to just play along, I raise the counter and head through to the hallway. My ankle is still hurting from the slip down the steps, but I try to hide that as much as possible. The last thing I want is to show weakness.

"Like I said," she continues, "it's just for one night. To be honest, my plans are pretty fluid and it was kinda last-minute for me to come to Canterbury at all. I mean, this morning I didn't even..."

Her voice trails off.

She looks tired. Exhausted, even.

"I'll show you to your room," I tell her, turning and heading toward the stairs. My ankle sends a sharp flicker of pain up through my leg, causing me to almost stumble, but I manage to hold myself together and keep going. I doubt she noticed a thing.

"Thank you," she mutters.

I don't even bother offering to help with her suitcase. I carried the damn thing up myself earlier, so she can do the same. Already, I can hear her puffing and panting a little, and I can't deny that I like the thought of her struggling. Glancing over my shoulder, I see that from the outside at least the suitcase looks to be a perfect facsimile of my own. There's no way anyone else in the world knows what I've been lugging about, but it's perfectly possible that – in order to make this little charade as realistic as possible – she's loaded her case down so that it's heavy as hell. In which case, I hope she enjoys the aching arms.

"Nice plant," she gasps finally.

Stopping, I turn and see that she's taking a rest. Looking down at the plant, I feel a flicker of itchiness running up my face, as if to remind me of the irritation that forced me to use these infernal bandages in the first place.

"Yeah, you'd think so," I grumble under my breath, kicking the pot gently with my bare foot and making a mental note to toss the plant out into the snow before I leave this miserable place. I'm tempted to throw it out right now, but I quickly remind myself that I need to act normal, so I turn and start limping to the top of the stairs.

Behind me, the girl is bumping her suitcase slowly and laboriously up each step. I swear to God, it's hard to believe how much she's puffing and panting.

"You have a really nice place here," she gasps.

Whatever.

Figuring that I need to get her into room four, I unlock the door and push it open. Having only grabbed my suitcase five or ten minutes ago, I step inside and find that I left the place looking pretty much pristine.

After all, I never got a chance to use the bed, or really to unpack, so the fusty smell is still very much present. In fact, as the girl hauls her suitcase across the threshold and over to the bed, I can't help leaning back against the wall and watching her with a hint of pity. She might look and sound exactly like me, but she's clearly weaker and more annoying.

I need to figure her out.

"Thank you so much for letting me stay," she says, heading over to the window once she's dropped her suitcase. She takes a moment to look out, and after a few seconds I realize she's looking down at the alley.

"Watch out for that place," I mumble.

She turns to me. "I'm sorry, what was -"

"Nothing," I add, figuring that the last thing I need is a long, complex conversation. "Ignore me. I didn't say anything."

"Okay, but -"

"Let's see how far you're willing to push this," I mutter, tossing the key onto the bed and then heading to the door.

"What time is breakfast?" she asks.

"Seven. Eight. Ten. Something like that."

My ankle is hurting more than ever as I make my way onto the landing. I feel I should say something, maybe just a little hint to let her know that I'm onto whatever game she's playing, but I'm honestly not sure where to begin. When I get to the top of the stairs, I realize I can hear her bumping around in her room, and I turn to look at the open door. I've just about had enough of this game and I'm tempted to march right in there and demand to know what she's up to, but somehow I hold back. I need to play this cool.

After a moment, the girl appears in the doorway, looking distinctly uncomfortable.

"I think I just need to sleep," she tells me, clearly poised to close the door. "I'm going to go to bed."

"Of course you are," I reply, holding my tongue.

"I'm sorry?"

I shrug, and again the bandages rustle loudly. I should try not to shrug again. The noise is irritating.

"We have food in the basement," I continue, figuring I need to play along for a little while longer, just to see how she reacts. "Late-night snacks, that kind of thing. There's a tea and coffee machine. Sometimes people..."

I pause, feeling as if maybe I should just leave her to do her own thing. She'll trip up eventually. She has to.

"You get the idea," I add finally. "There are biscuits too."

"Is that the bathroom?" she asks.

I glance at the glass-paneled door, and then I turn and nod again. Damn, I need to remember to stop doing that. Every time I nod, the bandages rustle loudly, and I think I'm dislodging some of the lotion. Patches of flesh on my left cheek are starting to itch again.

"Okay, thanks," she says, clearly feeling uncomfortable. "Goodnight, then," she adds, before swinging the door shut, leaving me alone on the landing.

Now what?

She's in my room, pretending to be me, and I have no idea how to react. There's still a part of me that wants to go and knock on that door and demand answers. In my mind's eye, I picture myself pinning her to the wall and wrapping my hands around her throat, demanding answers. She might think she's smart and resilient, but I could quickly show her which of us is *really* the tough one, and then she'd sing like a church mouse on Sunday. At the same time, I'm worried that I'd only be falling right into *their* trap, whoever *they* happen to be. Or I'd be succumbing to a whole new level of my delusion.

I should just get out of here.

This B&B is insane.

Taking a deep breath, I realize I've been standing here for a couple of minutes now. A moment later, I spot a flicker of movement in the keyhole that leads into room four, and to my shock I see that the girl is staring out at me. Startled, I turn and scamper down the stairs, although I stop once I'm just around the corner.

A moment later, I hear a door swinging shut on the ground floor. For a few seconds, it occurs to me that perhaps somebody just went into the office, which I guess means that the real landlady might have shown up again. I'm not sure whether I should avoid her or go and demand answers.

Not knowing what to do, I remain poised halfway up the stairs, next to the evil plant. My mind is racing and I genuinely have no idea where to go. If I head back up, I risk running into that little faker again, but if I go down I'll surely bump into the landlady. At the same time, my clothes are still drying in the office, and my suitcase is there too with all my cash inside, so it's not like I can just bolt for the front door and run away into the night. I don't even know the time right now, but I figure morning has to come fairly soon. I already feel like I've been in this place forever.

"Dear God," I whisper, crouching down and leaning against the wall. "I've never believed in you before, but if you could get me out of this madhouse, I could definitely see my way to believing in you and being a better person. I know I've made a few mistakes lately, but -"

Mistakes?

That's the understatement of the century.

Then again, if God *does* exist, I'm sure he's seen every move I've made. In which case, there's probably a whole lot of extra punishment lined up for me. I mean, one thing I've learned lately is that I am definitely *not* a good person.

I'm a liar and a thief.

I lean my head back against the wall, and it occurs to me that maybe this is all a big cosmic hint. Maybe this is the universe telling me to go home, to confess to everything and face justice. It's not like I can just keep running for the rest of my life, and I'd probably feel better about myself if I turned myself in rather than waiting until I'm caught. Besides, it's the right thing to do.

I just don't know if I'm that brave.

The police would get involved. They probably are already. I might even go to jail.

"Why am I such an idiot?" I whisper under the bandages. "Why do I always -"

Suddenly I hear a door opening upstairs, on the landing. I freeze, worried that somebody is about to come to the stairs and spot me, but a moment later I hear another door swinging open. In fact, I think maybe while I was lost in my thoughts I heard a couple more bumps as well, although I'm not entirely sure of that.

"I'm sorry," I hear the girl with a whiny version of my voice say finally, "I thought..."

In the distance, there's the sound of someone splashing about in the bathroom.

"No," I whisper. "No way, this isn't -"

"I can do this in the morning," the girl continues, "I just -"

"Nonsense," I hear Jude reply brightly. "Come on, don't fret. I won't be long in there. And trust me, I've been staying here long enough by now to know that there's *never* not a queue. If you wanna get into that bathroom any time in the next twenty-four hours, you'd better get your butt over here and stake your spot."

Seriously?

This part is happening again? Is Jude in on the whole thing too? There's no other possible explanation. I'd assumed it was just the crazy lookalike who was trying to freak me out, but a sense of fear starts spreading through my chest as I realize that everybody in this entire B&B might be playing some kind of long, drawn-out prank on me.

"Oh, look at you," Jude continues with a laugh. "Like a deer in the headlights."

I stay where I am, still crouching on the stairs, and listen as she goes on and on. She certainly loves talking, but I'm more and more certain that she's saying *exactly* what she said to me earlier, word for word. I mean, that's not possible, it can't be, but I can't deny what I'm hearing.

"Now come over here," she says finally, "and claim your spot before somebody else comes and jumps in ahead of you. My name's Jude, by the way. I didn't catch yours."

Figuring that I really don't need to stay crouched here, listening to a re-run of everything that happened earlier, I quietly get to my feet and make my way past the plant, heading down to the hallway. Sure enough, the door to the office is shut, and I'm fairly sure I left it open a few minutes ago when I left to take the fake version of me up to her room. I glance toward the stairs that lead down to the basement, and I think I can hear a series of faint bumps down there.

Hurrying to the office, I push the door open and make my way to where my clothes are drying on the chairs. They're still a little damp, but right now that's the least important thing in the world. All that matters is that I get the hell out of this B&B and never, ever come back.

"Cold night."

Startled, I let out a terrified shriek, losing my footing as I turn and slam down to the ground. There's a man standing calmly at the window, watching the snow while holding his hands together behind his back. After a moment he turns and smiles at me.

Lloyd. What the hell is Lloyd doing in here?

CHAPTER SIX

"HE'S OUT THERE, YOU know," he continues, parting the net curtains again and looking out at the snowy street. "I can feel it in the air. I can almost taste it. I don't know how that works, but I can just tell that the Snowman isn't far away. This night is absolutely perfect for him."

Still on the floor, I stare at him. I'd been hoping that everyone was safely in bed by now, but a moment later I spot a clock on top of the old television.

"Quarter to eleven?" I whisper, sitting up. "No way, it has to be more than -"

"There!" Lloyd says suddenly, tapping the window. "I saw someone!"

I turn to him, while still trying to make sense of this madness, and I see that he's craning his neck as he tries to look further along the street.

"I saw him!" he hisses, his voice filled with excitement.

"You saw *who*?" I ask, wincing as I get to my feet. It's not just my ankle that hurts now. When I fell, I landed on my right hip, and I think I might have damaged something. At the very least, I'm gonna have a hell of a bruise. "Lloyd, what are you doing in here?"

"I'm sorry," he replies, still peering out the window. "I didn't mean to intrude, but I *did* knock. I think you were upstairs at the time, showing a new arrival to her room. I'm afraid curiosity got the better of me and I just *had* to come and use your window for a few minutes. Like I said, I don't know how, but I just felt certain that the Snowman was going to run past. And sure enough, he did. Off on another of his deadly hunts, I shouldn't doubt."

"Lloyd -"

"I mean, all I saw was a shadow," he adds, turning to me, "but who else would dare go out there on a night like this? It must have been him!"

I limp over to the television and look at the clock again. Sure enough, it still shows the time as being a little after quarter to eleven, and the second hand is ticking healthily. It has to be wrong, I know that, but for a moment I feel as if this entire place is twisting its way into my mind and infecting me with its own dose of madness.

"Lloyd," I say cautiously, "do you happen to have the time?"

"The time?"

"Humor me."

I turn just as he checks his watch.

"Well, it's 10.46," he tells me. "Your clock there

isn't wrong."

"It can't be 10.46," I reply, starting to feel a little faint. "It has to be more like three or four, maybe even five in the morning."

"Does it?"

"Of course it does!"

He furrows his brow.

"What's going on here?" I continue, trying not to panic. "I was outside, after Matilda ran off, and then..."

My voice fades as I think back to the sight of the fake version of me. I guess she's upstairs somewhere, going through the motions of pretending to *be* me, and the thought is enough to send a shudder through my chest. After a moment, I limp to the little mirror over the sink behind the door, and when I look at my reflection I'm shocked to see that I look *exactly* like the landlady. I'm wearing her gown, and I hadn't realized it at the time but now I realize that I really covered my entire head with those bandages.

Reaching up, I gently ease the bandages aside, revealing my rash-covered, reddened face. I stare at myself for a moment, before sliding the bandages back into place.

This can't be happening.

"I suppose the others will be ready soon," Lloyd mutters suddenly. "I've got to admit, it'll be difficult to keep my mind focused on anything else. Sometimes I think I'm rather obsessed by the case of the Snowman, but it's all just so fascinating! Mark my words, somebody is going to die tonight. The Snowman will have his victim, regardless of what the others might think."

I turn to him.

"The others?" I ask cautiously.

"Down in the breakfast room." He chuckles. "Well, we call it the breakfast room, but I'm not sure why. We spend more time there at night than we ever do in the mornings. Perhaps we should rename it the games room, or the night room." He pauses, before heading to the door. "The funny thing is, I can't remember the last time I saw a ray of sunshine. Some nights feel much longer than others, don't they?"

"Do they?" I ask.

"Are you alright?" he continues, turning to me. "I know this might sound odd, but I can't shake the feeling that you might be looking a little pale under all those bandages. In fact, you've seemed out-of-sorts ever since you came in just now."

I stare at him, and for a moment I can't help wondering how much he knows.

"How long have you been here?" I ask finally.

"I beg your pardon?"

"At the B&B. How long have you been staying here?"

"Oh, a long time now," he replies with a sheepish smile, as he slips his hands into his pockets. "Almost as long as you, I'd wager. Maybe even longer."

"And how long do you think *I've* been here."

He chuckles. "Well that's a queer question."

Glancing over at the chairs in the corner, I see that my wet clothes from earlier are still drying. I could probably slip into them right now, but I don't see my suitcase anywhere and I need to take it with me. I need the money, so I can catch a train, and so that I still have the option of taking it all home and turning myself in. Heading over to the chairs, I feel my shirt and find that it's almost completely dry. A fraction of a second later, I hear a faint bump from upstairs, and I look at the ceiling just in time to hear a set of footsteps.

"Somebody going into the bathroom, no doubt," Lloyd mutters.

"Where's my suitcase?" I ask.

"I beg your pardon?"

"My suitcase! It's important! I can't leave until I've found it!"

"Well, I can't say that I know," he mutters. "Have you checked your room? That's where I'd put mine."

Ignoring him, I head to the door and peer out into the hallway. There's definitely somebody up there, although after a moment I hear a door swinging shut. Now the entire house seems rather quiet, almost *too* quiet, and I feel a tightening sense of curiosity rippling through my chest as I step over to the foot of the stairs and look up toward the plant.

"Are you okay?" Lloyd asks.

I pause, before turning to him. "Did -"

Suddenly there's a loud bump from one of the rooms above us.

"Sounds like that came from the bathroom," Lloyd mutters.

Without a second thought, I start making my way up the stairs, while taking great care to not go anywhere near the plant. By the time I get to the landing, my heart is pounding, and I see that the bathroom door has been left slightly ajar with the light still on inside and the sound of the shower running. There's no sign of anyone, but I'm starting to think back now to my experiences earlier tonight and I distinctly remember finding the red-stained man in the empty bathtub, and then...

And then...

Stepping over to the door, I gently push it open. It creaks a little, revealing first the sink and the towel rack, and then the empty but running shower cabinet, and finally the sight of me, or rather the girl who looks like me, unconscious on the floor.

I freeze, trying to work out what to do next.

"Hello?" I whisper.

No reply.

I take a deep breath, before making my way cautiously into the room. The girl is still down there on the floor, as if she slipped in the puddles of bloodied water and hit her head on the floor. I remember that, and I remember waking up later with Jude standing over me, but obviously I don't remember anything from the period when I was knocked out. Now, stepping closer to the girl, I can't help wondering whether maybe this isn't a trap after all. Or if it *is* a trap, maybe it's one that involves a little more than just some scrappy doppelganger who was sent to fool me. Stopping and looking down at the girl, I tilt my head slightly, trying to get a better look at her.

It's really me.

I mean, I've never seen myself when I'm unconscious before, but I really, truly think this is me.

"No," I whisper, feeling another shudder run through my chest. "It can't be."

I pause, before crouching next to her. I'm worried about waking her, but then again I know that I wasn't woken earlier when this happened to me. But what does that mean? Does it mean I can't wake her now, even if I try? Is she simply pretending to be unconscious, in an attempt to drive me out of my mind? Or did she really hit her head and really knock herself out? I stare at her for a moment longer, before looking over at the side of the white porcelain bathtub.

Getting to my feet, I immediately see that the red-stained naked man is still in place, still curled on his side at the bottom of the tub. Transfixed by the sight, I edge around the side of the bath, hoping against hope that I might spot a 'Made in China' label somewhere on the spotty, pocked flesh, or perhaps a seam where some kind of dummy has been sewn together. The more I look at the body, however, the more I start to realize that it's an actual human.

"Oh," a familiar voice says suddenly. "She *did* drain the water."

Turning, I'm startled to see Jude standing in the doorway.

"I asked her if she could refrain," she continues, "but perhaps she didn't hear me."

She comes over to join me, and then she stops to look down at the girl on the floor.

"Poor thing must have had a fright when she saw

him. I can't imagine what went through her head." She sighs, before setting the towels on a chair next to the tub. "I don't suppose you could be a honey and help me move him, could you? I wouldn't ask, but he was piling on the pounds in his final days. Probably comfort-eating as he dealt with the pain. If I can just get him to our room, I can lay him out and treat him with the respect he deserves, rather than leaving him here like this for everyone to see. He wouldn't want people to start talking."

"What..."

Taking a step back, I stare at the man in the bathtub for a moment longer before stumbling, almost tripping over the unconscious girl's arm. I steady myself, but my heart is still pounding.

"What happened here?" I ask.

"I told you it was what he wanted," she replies. "My Herb was a complicated man, that's for sure."

"What did you do?" I stammer. "Is he... Is that a..."

My voice trails off as I continue to stare at the body.

"Let's just give him some dignity," she replies, grabbing one of the towels and unfolding it before laying it gently over the man's face. She takes another and covers his side, and then she places one more over his legs until only his hands and feet are showing. "This is how he would have wanted it to be. He was a very proper man, you know. He wouldn't have wanted people poking about in his private affairs. Especially with the boy to consider."

She sighs.

"Oh," she adds after a moment. "That poor boy."

"What boy?" I ask.

She pauses, with tears filling her eyes, and then she reaches down to grab the man's wrists.

"Can you take his ankles, honey?" she asks.

Figuring that I should at least try, I take hold of his ankles and brace myself. This Herb guy looks pretty heavy, but I guess I'm hardly in a position to deny Jude's request.

"You've mentioned a boy a couple of times now," I point out. "I haven't seen a boy since I got here."

"One," she says after a moment, as if she didn't hear me at all. "Ready? Two. Three. Lift!"

We both lift, and we just about manage to get him out of the bath. At the last moment, my left hand slips and I almost drop him ass-first straight on top of the unconscious girl, but I manage to keep hold at the last moment. Trying not to let it seem too obvious that I'm struggling, I carefully help carry the man over to the door, while making sure that I don't slip again in the pale red water that's still splashed all over the floor.

"The coast's clear!" Jude gasps, after peering out at the landing, and then we stumble out with the body swinging between us.

A moment later, however, I spot the timid woman creeping down the stairs. As usual, she stops as soon as she sees that she has company, and then she starts making her way back up, while keeping her eyes fixed on us until she disappears into the gloom.

"Who's that woman?" I gasp, struggling with the

man's weight.

"Oh, ignore Betty," Jude replies. "She keeps herself to herself. She's barely even here, really."

"Barely here?"

"Make sure you don't drop Herb," she continues. "That's the important thing. He wouldn't like to be dropped."

It only takes half a minute to get him to room three, and finally we lower him onto the bed, where his body immediately leaves several red marks on the crisp, blindingly-white sheets.

My arms are aching as I take a step back, and I feel more than a little out of breath.

Jude sits on the side of the bed and pulls towels from over Herb's face, and then she reaches down and gently strokes his cheek. For a moment, she seems utterly lost in thought, and I watch as tears start trickling down her face. She looks utterly heartbroken, and it's clear that she's struggling to keep from bursting into a full sobbing mess. Finally she spits on one of the towels and then uses it to gently wipe some of the blood from his flesh.

"You must think this is so bizarre," she whimpers finally, as her bottom lip starts trembling.

I open my mouth to reply, but I'm not sure what to say.

I mean, she's right.

"Herb and I had so much fun," she continues, wiping some of the tears away. "Ours wasn't the kind of marriage that slowly fades into routine. We stayed so alive and so alert, even after we became parents. Even when Herb's health problems began, we never let things get us down. He hid the effects for as long as possible, but slowly he began to deteriorate more and more, until the shaking and the confusion started to show on a daily basis. Guests began to notice while he was checking them in. I took on more responsibilities around the place, but that only made him feel bad. He started talking about wanting me to be free. About wanting to set the boy and me free."

She falls silent, still stroking his face as more red water stains the sheets.

"Maybe I should leave you guys alone," I say after a moment, slowly backing toward the door.

"I knew his condition was becoming terminal," she adds. "We both did, but we thought he had a little longer. I think maybe he started hiding the doctor's words from me. When he said he had years left, it was probably only months. And when he said it was months..." She pauses, still staring at him as tears drip from her cheeks and land on his bare face, where they continue to trickle down to his chin. "Everything he did was because he was worried about our little family. He was trying to do the right thing, even if he got it all a little wrong. I just wish he could have been more open with me at the end. If I'd known what he was thinking, I could have saved us all so much pain."

I stare at her.

"I don't understand," I tell her finally.

She turns to me.

"I don't get it," I continue. "I just -"

Before I can finish, I realize I can hear someone

sobbing nearby. I turn and look back toward the doorway, but there's no sign of anyone. Still, I can definitely hear what sounds like a child quietly weeping, so I step over to the door and look out at the landing.

The sobbing stops.

I wait, listening to the silence of the building, and then I turn back to see that Jude is stroking her husband's face.

"I don't understand," I tell her again, feeling the hairs starting to rise on the back of my neck. "This doesn't make sense."

She sniffs back some more tears.

"Well," she says finally, "lucky you, that's all I can say. Lucky, lucky you. Because if it *did* make sense, that'd mean you were... Well, it'd mean you were like me and Herb, and I don't think I'd wish that on anybody. You should thank your lucky stars that you can't get your head around this. Trust me, I take no comfort from the fact that it makes sense to me. I wish I could be shocked, or that I didn't believe it, but I do. I've lived through it. But I had no choice, because I wanted to be with my dear, sweet Herb. I just wish that, as parents, we'd both done a better job. So much of this is our fault."

She leans down and kisses the side of his face.

"We should have stayed around for the boy," she whispers.

I wait for her to continue.

"What boy?" I ask, feeling a shiver pass through my chest.

"The poor boy," she sobs, placing her face against Herb's shoulder. "One of us should have stayed for him, at least. I suppose it should have been me. Without us, he was almost wild."

"What boy?" I ask again. "You keep..."

My voice trails off. This whole situation still feels way too bizarre for me to even begin to understand, but at the same time it's at least not quite as crazy as what's going on in the bathroom with the girl who looks like me. My heart is thudding in my chest and I feel like I've just stepped into an even weirder side-world that makes absolutely no sense at all. At the same time, I can't deny that Jude seems genuinely horrified by her husband's death, and I can't deny that she appears to have enjoyed the kind of love that I've never felt in all my life.

Suddenly I see that there are thick, knotted wounds on Herb's wrists, just like the wounds I saw on Jude before.

"What happened to him?" I whisper. "Did he..."

My voice trails off for a moment.

"I have to go and do something," I stammer finally, turning and hurrying out of the room.

Once I've pulled the door shut, I pause for a moment and look toward the bathroom. My heart is pounding, but I'm starting to think that no matter how crazy I might be right now, there's no way my mind is responsible for all the madness around me. A moment later, I'm surprised to realize that I can hear someone bumping around in the bathroom, and suddenly I see Mrs. Denham shuffling out.

"There's a girl in there," the old lady tells me, clearly not very impressed. "She's on the floor, right next to the bath. It's not right. The standards around here are quite awful. I was hoping to use the facilities before I went down to play cards with my husband in the breakfast room."

Stepping over to the bathroom door, I look through and see that the girl is still right where I left her.

"I tried to clean up the mess," Mrs. Denham continues, "but there was so much of it. Somebody had spilled everywhere. I know you can't completely control what your guests get up to, but I *do* wish you could have a word with some of them. Doesn't that girl have a perfectly good bed waiting for her?"

"She does," I whisper, staring at the girl for a moment longer before turning to Mrs. Denham and seeing that she's shuffling slowly toward the top of the stairs. Reaching up, I adjust the bandages so that I can see better.

Mrs. Denham grips the railing, but I swear she looks far too frail to make it down unaided.

"Wait!" I call out, hurrying over and taking hold of her arm. "Let me help you!"

"My husband went down a little early," she explains as we start slowly making our way downstairs. "He wanted to see if he could get that infernal coffee machine warmed up before we start our game. I don't mean to complain so much, but would it not be possible to acquire a simple kettle for the breakfast room? I honestly can't understand why the people who run this place feel the need to have such a complicated machine when a kettle would suffice without nearly so much fuss."

"That's a good point," I tell her, guiding her around the turn halfway down the stairs. "Someone should look into it."

"Of course, he'd been an ambulance driver for quite some time, and I don't think he entirely enjoyed his work."

I open my mouth to reply, before realizing that I have no idea what she's talking about.

"What did you say?" I ask cautiously.

"So when he saw that awful woman again," she continues, "I think something just snapped in him. But he still wouldn't have done what he did, not if she hadn't been so shrill and insistent. Apparently she told him to keep working on the poor man's body, even long after it was clear he was dead. She threatened to sue him, and to get him fired, if he didn't perform more and more chest compressions. The upshot of *that* was that he ended up crushing her father's chest and forcing pipes down his throat, all by the side of the road and with her shrieking at him. Such an awful, awful girl. She was demanding that he torture the poor man in his final moments."

"Um, okay," I reply, still trying to figure out what she means. I think maybe she's not quite right in the head, and she's telling me the middle of some random story. Without the beginning, the middle doesn't make much sense at all.

"In some ways, I don't blame him for what he did next," she adds. "He must have been at breaking point and he just snapped. He told her there was only one thing left to try, and that she had to be the one who did it. He told her it was the last chance to save her father's life. And since she was in such a terrible state, and since she didn't recognize a lowly ambulance driver... Well, she did it! I shouldn't laugh, really I shouldn't. I just can't help it!"

"Um..."

"And that plant is horrid!" she says. "It's the ugliest, most foul thing I've seen in my life!"

"Absolutely," I reply, although she's leaning heavily against me and – in the process – she just so happens to be steering me directly *into* the plant. "Just go a little that way," I tell her, struggling to keep myself clear. "Can you -"

I let out a gasp as my hand brushes against one of the fronds, and of course there's a flash of pain a moment later.

Fortunately, I quickly lead Mrs. Denham to the second set of steps, and we start making our way down. My hand is becoming more painful by the second, but I figure I don't have time right now to go and apply more lotion. Instead, I lead the elderly lady to the next flight of stairs, and I can already hear voices drifting up from down in the breakfast room.

"There she is!" Lloyd exclaims a few minutes later, once we get to the breakfast room's door. "Major Denham, your dear wife has finally made it down, ably assisted by our delightful host! Now the games can begin!"

He turns to Matilda, who of course is sitting in the far corner with her nose in her copy of *The Wind in the Willows*. Next to her on the table, there's a white bowl containing sachets of ketchup and mayonnaise.

"Now we just need to find a fourth player," Lloyd continues, "and we're all set for our evening's entertainment!"

"I'm not playing!" Matilda says dourly, turning to the next page.

As the elderly lady goes to join her husband, I take a step back. Bumping against the trolley, I turn and see some white porcelain mugs. My throat is dry, so I grab one of the mugs and fill it with water from a nearby jug.

"I don't mean to complain," Lloyd says, lowering his voice as he turns to me, "but the coffee machine -"

"Isn't working properly?" I ask, remembering all the fuss from earlier. "Sure. I get it."

I take a sip of water.

"Has anyone seen a suitcase?" I mutter after a moment, turning to them. "I really need to find my suitcase."

"I think it might be the water pressure," Major Denham continues. "If you just check the boiler room, you'll most likely find that the dial has been turned the wrong way."

I stare at him. Is he serious? Does he really think I'm going to go poking about in some boiler room, trying to find a way to fix the goddamn coffee machine?

"I need to find my suitcase," I tell him. "So I can get out of here."

"It's right behind you," he continues, rather plaintively.

Turning, I see that sure enough there's a door with the named BOILER ROOM in small letters. I noticed the room earlier, of course, although I didn't give it much thought. Still, the idea of going in there is ludicrous, even if it somehow fits with the rest of the insanity that seems to pervade this entire building.

"I know you usually only use the room to store your stocks of lotion," Lloyd adds, "but still, the coffee machine has been out of action since... I actually can't remember it ever working properly, and tonight is such a cold and snowy evening. Don't you think you could bring yourself to take a quick look?"

I turn to him. "Where's my suitcase?"

He furrows his brow.

"It was in the office," I continue, "but now I can't find it."

"Well..." He pauses. "I suppose it might be in the lost property box."

"Where's that?"

"Well, it's in the boiler room."

Sighing, I realize that one way or another, I seem destined to go into that infernal boiler room. Turning and heading across the corridor, I push the door open and step into a very dark and very warm room, with the only light coming from a slit-shaped window at the very top of the far wall. I take a step forward, while fumbling for a light-switch, but a moment later the door swings shut and I'm left alone in darkness.

There's a table nearby, barely visible as my eyes adjust to the darkness, so I set the coffee mug down before stumbling forward. I hold my hands out, to make sure I don't hit anything, and after a moment I feel the splinter-covered wood of a supporting post. Making my way around the post, I continue to head across the room, only to bump against another post. Stopping, I take a deep breath of cold air, while trying to figure out exactly which way I should go next. So far, there's no sign of anything that remotely resembles a lost property box, and I certainly can't see my suitcase.

"Come on," I mutter, hoping that my eyes will adjust a little better to the darkness. "Where are you? I want to get out of this place."

I take a couple more steps forward, while muttering a few choice curses under my breath, but suddenly I bump against something on the floor and I fall forward, letting out a pained gasp as I slam down onto the concrete floor. At the last moment, I hit my head on the side of a metal railing.

And I'm knocked clean out again.

CHAPTER SEVEN

"DAMN IT!" I HISS suddenly, rolling onto my side. My head is throbbing and I feel a little dizzy, but the worst of the pain quickly passes. "What the -"

I feel decidedly groggy, but I have no idea how long I spent unconscious. Seconds maybe. Minutes. Hours.

Hauling myself up, I stagger forward until I spot a patch of moonlight falling across a set of metal steps, and I take a moment to sit down. All around me, the air is sweltering, and there's a large boiler lurking in the shadows. This room might be all the way down in the basement, but there's a small window at the top of one of the walls, and after a moment I see that these steps lead up to another door. There's a glass panel on the door, and snow is falling outside, so I guess the door somehow leads out into the yard that backs onto the alley.

"Great," I mutter, before spotting a large crate nearby.

Peering inside, hoping that I might have found the lost property collection and that my suitcase might be nearby, I see nothing more than a pile of newspapers. I grab the top paper and see that the front page is filled with a story about the so-called Snowman killer.

"Deadly Snowman strikes again," I whisper, reading out loud as I unfold the yellowed page. "Police in Canterbury confirmed last night that 23-year-old Elizabeth Waddington was indeed killed by the mysterious killer known only as the Snowman, ending days of speculation. Ever since Miss Waddington was found brutally murdered in the snow, near the city's Castle Crown B&B..."

My voice trails off for a moment.

"Huh," I mutter, before continuing to read. "Rumors have been swirling that the Snowman might have struck again. Now that those rumors have been proved true, police are facing questions about why they still haven't caught the killer. Elizabeth is his fifth victim in a little under a decade, with all the murders having taken place in snowy weather. Representatives for the city's night-watch patrol team, a voluntary organization, say they can only do so much."

I set the paper aside and take another from the crate, only to find that it's even older, dating from the late 1990's. Water seems to have leaked into the crate, smudging a lot of the words, so it takes a moment before I can find a section I'm able to read.

"Is the pattern real," I read, "or is it just a coincidence that the killer only strikes when snow is on the ground? Does a madman, snarling and lusting for blood, really stalk our quaint streets, searching for his next victim? If so, where does he lurk between murders?"

I put the paper down and take yet another from the crate. This time, I see a map that apparently shows the locations of all the victims, and I can't help noticing that they're all within a few blocks of this very B&B. Beneath the map, there's a panel that explains a murder has taken place on every snowy night in the city for almost thirty years. There's also a section where a psychiatrist has been asked to give his opinion, but most of the text has been torn away and water damage has destroyed the rest.

Looking down at the crate again, I can't help wondering why someone would want to keep so many cuttings about such a grizzly set of incidents.

Getting to my feet, I start hunting once more for my suitcase. I guess somebody cleared it away, thinking it had been abandoned, but in the back of my mind I'm starting to worry that maybe it's been stolen. There's more than £26,000 cash in that suitcase, and I need to find it so I can...

I pause for a moment.

So I can what?

Until a few hours ago, I was planning to go on the run with the money. Now, however, I've begun to realize that I can't possibly do something so stupid and wrong. I have to find the money and take it home, and hand it back to its rightful owner. I'll have to pay for moment of weakness, I know that, but at least I'll know I'm doing the right thing. First, though, I need to actually get the suitcase and the money back. Going home with an apology but without the money would never be enough. I took that money from good people and they need to get it back.

Once I've checked the basement, I realize that the suitcase has to be somewhere else in the building. I could go back upstairs the way I came, past the breakfast room, but the last thing I want is to bump into Lloyd and the others again so instead I turn and start limping up the metal stairs, ignoring the pain in my ankle as I get closer to the door. I know I should go back through to the others, but my head is spinning and I'm starting to think that I'd rather just go out the back way, head around the building and in through the front door, and then find the suitcase before leaving forever without saying goodbye. I have a key to the front door in the pocket of my gown, and I'm relieved to find that the back door has been left unlocked.

Just as I start to turn the handle, however, I hear something clattering against the wall outside.

I freeze, trying not to panic and focusing instead of the chance that the noise was caused by a gust of wind. A moment later, however, I hear another bump, followed by a set of footsteps trampling through the snow. I immediately think back to my encounter out there earlier, when some kind of figure pinned me down, and then I realize the footsteps are on the other side of the door. Spotting a rust old key in the lock, I turn it quickly, locking the door just a fraction of a second before the handle is suddenly grabbed and turned from outside.

Whoever's out there, they try several times to force the door open, and then I hear a faint, annoyed grunt.

I hold my breath and wait.

Silence.

Suddenly something slams into the other side of the door. Gasping, I step back, almost falling down the stairs. A moment later the door is hit again, shuddering in its frame. Whatever's out there, it sounds very angry and very keen to get inside. Still holding my breath, I realize I can hear a faint but persistent sniffing sound, almost as if the creature has picked up my scent. I take another step back, just before the door is hit for a third time. The impact is even harder this time, and I hear a loud grunt from outside before everything falls still again.

Still not daring to move, I stare at the door.

It's gone.

Whatever was out there, it must have -

Suddenly there's an even larger impact, causing the door to shake. And then, just as I'm about to turn and run, I hear footsteps trudging away through the snow. Whatever that thing is, it must have given up. It seemed strong, though. Real strong, almost strong enough to knock down a door, and I can't help worrying that something appeared to be very keen to break into the B&B. In fact, as I take another step back from the door, I can't help thinking back to all that talk of the Snowman. I mean, maybe someone just wanted to get inside in a hurry for some perfectly innocent reason, but I don't think I want to take any chances.

I make my way back down the steps and then I start fumbling back across the darkened boiler room. I briefly try to find the coffee mug I left in here earlier, before giving up and heading toward the lines of light that show the edges of the exit.

"Don't panic," I mutter under my breath, trying to remind myself that I have no proof it was the infamous Snowman trying to get inside. "It's probably nothing."

I can hear voices nearby, so I guess there are more people in the breakfast room. Taking a deep breath, I brush some fragments of dirt from the front of my night-gown before pulling the door open. Still feeling a little freaked out by whoever was trying to get into the building, I make my way back to the breakfast room, only to stop as soon as I see that the other girl – the girl who looks like me – is up and about again, and she's talking to the others. As the boiler room's door swings shut behind me, I reach up and check that my bandages are still in place.

"The coffee machine is still on the fritz," Lloyd tells me. "I tried turning it off and on again. Whatever you did, it hasn't made a spot of difference."

I stare at him, convinced that he has to be joking, and then I look over at the coffee machine.

"You want to get that thing fixed," he adds.

For a moment, all I want to do is take the goddamn coffee machine, rip it away from the wall, and throw it to the ground. I'm tempted to give direct action a try, but I guess I'd only end up seeming completely psychotic. Still, as Lloyd starts talking to the other girl, I look over at the machine and start wondering whether by some miracle I might be able to get it working again. Lost in thought, I quickly come back to the same conclusion as earlier, which is that the damn thing most likely needs a good kicking.

"Do *you* remember how many nights I've been here?" Lloyd asks suddenly.

Turning, I realize he was talking to me. I pause, before shaking my head. The rustling bandages are becoming seriously annoying.

"Sshh!" Matilda hisses, placing a finger against her lips.

I turn to her, and she glares at Lloyd for a moment before turning and staring straight at me. Something about her gaze seems rather uncanny, as if she's trying to see through my eyes and into my mind, and I can't help feeling as if she's in possession of a sea of shimmering rage that exists just beneath the surface, waiting to explode.

She's fiddling with a ketchup packet, too, as if she can find no other way to express her seething anger.

"I wonder if he's found his latest victim yet," Lloyd says, his voice filled with wonder as he looks up toward the ceiling. "Even if there's no news, he *might* have struck, and the body is simply awaiting discovery. Or perhaps he's merely tracking her through the snow, waiting for his chance. Or I suppose it's possible that he's still on the lookout, still waiting for some timid little mouse to scurry out from one of the city's doors. Matilda, for example. If I were him, I'd start near the cathedral. Good hunting ground and -"

"For God's sake!" Matilda yells suddenly, getting to her feet. "Can't you just shut up?!?"

Startled, I step back and almost knock the entire trolley over. As I steady myself, I can't help thinking that I should have been ready for that, that I should have remembered from last time that Matilda was going to blow her lid after Lloyd wittered on for a while. I still don't quite know what's going on here, but it's quite clear that I'm stuck in some kind of reenactment of the night so far, albeit seeing things from another perspective. The whole thing has to be a trick, I know that, and I'm certainly not given to flights of fancy. At the same time, I still don't know how to begin explaining all of this. I just need to find my suitcase and get out of here. Even as Lloyd and Matilda argue, I find myself lost in thought, desperately trying to come up with an answer.

Wait, maybe the suitcase is in the -

"Shut up!" Matilda yells suddenly.

Startled again, I step back against the wall. I definitely should have remembered that second little outburst. And now, as Matilda starts really laying into Lloyd, my mind starts racing as I try to remember what happens next. If this all goes according to plan, they'll argue for a little while longer and then Matilda will storm out. Then she'll leave the building and run off, and eventually she'll play her silly little stunt in the alley with the ketchup. I watch for a moment, following every word of their disagreement, waiting to see if anything changes at all.

Finally, however, Matilda storms out in the exact same fashion as before. She still has a ketchup sachet in her right hand.

"Two of hearts," Major Denham announces proudly.

I should have remembered that, too. I need to pay attention. As the others continue to talk, I try to think of what might happen next. Turning to look at the coffee machine, I remember that last time I was here, it suddenly burst into life. There's no reason for that to happen right now, of course, although after a moment I suddenly spot a wire that looks to be loose at the back. Reaching down, I take hold of the wire and shove it back into its slot, giving it a twist for good measure.

The machine immediately starts grumbling and shuddering. Taking a step back, I watch with a sense of shock as water starts running from the spout, filling a cup.

"See?" Lloyd says finally. "Told you it'd get going eventually. It just takes a little time, that's all."

"Something tried to get into the building," I mumble under the bandages, before realizing that this whole situation is too much for me. "I'm getting out of here!"

With that, I turn and hurry out of the room, and I quickly start scrambling up the stairs until I reach the hallway on the ground floor. Just as I get there, however, I see that Matilda is heading toward the front door, marching with a great deal of purpose. As soon as she pulls the door open, a blast of cold air rushes through, ruffling her hair.

"Where are you going?" I call after her.

She turns to me. "Where do you think?" she

spits. "I'm going to prove to that asshole that there's no reason to be scared!"

"I wouldn't bother, if I were you," I reply, stepping closer. "Why don't you just stay in tonight? It looks pretty crazy out there."

"Are you like him?" she asks, with evident disdain. "Do you think we should all be hiding away, terrified of this Snowman monster?"

"Have you seen my suitcase?" I reply.

She scowls at me. "What?"

"Never mind," I tell her, figuring that maybe I can avoid the whole mess in the alley with the ketchup. "Listen, there's no point tempting fate. Ignore Lloyd, he talks a lot but I'm pretty sure most of it's just hot air."

"That's exactly the kind of thing I hate," she sneers. "It's not enough for him to cower in fear. He wants everyone else to do the same, too. He wants us all to stay down in that breakfast room, like it's some kind of air-raid shelter, hiding away from the world. And why? All because of some imagined monster that he swears is gonna come and get us! There's nothing out there!"

"I wouldn't be so sure about that," I tell her.

"Obviously he's tricked you too," she replies. "It's pitiful, really. But you know what they say, right? The only thing to fear is fear itself. So I'm gonna prove to Lloyd and the others, including you, that there's nothing out there in the snow waiting to get any of us!"

"I'm not sure you should be -"

Before I can get another word out, she hurries down the steps and out into the snow.

"Wait!"

I run to the door, but she's already wading through the thick snow, making her way toward the far end of the street.

"Matilda!" I shout. "Come back!"

Sighing, I realize I'm too late. Clearly she's set on her course, and it's not as if there's anything I can do to stop her. Then again, in theory I know *exactly* what'll happen to her, which in turn means that I know she'll be fine. Even if the Snowman really *is* out there somewhere hunting his latest victim, I know he won't chance upon Matilda, because I already know that she makes it back to the B&B just fine. She's annoying, sure, but it's not like her life is in danger. At least, I don't think so. To be honest, I'm struggling to keep all the different causes and effects in the right order.

Standing in the doorway for a moment, I watch as she disappears into the distance.

"Idiot," I mutter, thinking about her stupid trick with the ketchup. "Fine, just go and -"

Suddenly I spot a figure in the distance, hurrying through the snow. It's not Matilda, that's for sure, and I barely have time to register what I'm seeing before the figure disappears down another street. From this far, and with my bad eyesight, the figure looked like little more than a stick-limbed smudge, but I feel a flash of fear before reminding myself that I already know Matilda makes it back to the B&B without any trouble.

That figure was probably just some other fool who saw fit to go out into the snow. Or he was one of the night-watch people I've heard about. Maybe his lantern was just broken.

Forcing myself to stay calm, I turn and head back toward the office. Just as I'm about to go inside, however, I hear footsteps coming up from the basement. I freeze, trying not to panic, and then I scuttle over to the stairs and make my way up to the turn. Glancing back, I see the girl, the one who looks like me, heading cautiously toward the front door. I remain in place, too scared to move, and I watch as she leans out into the snowy night.

"Hello?" she shouts.

"It's not me," I whisper. "It can't -"

Suddenly the phone starts ringing. The girl turns, but I duck around the corner just in time, and a moment later I hear more footsteps coming up from the basement. It'll be Lloyd, I'm sure of it.

"I think somebody went outside," the girl says. Her voice sounds as whiny, nasal and irritating as ever.

"Is nobody else here to answer that?" Lloyd asks.

I hear more footsteps, followed by the sound of the phone's receiver being lifted from the cradle.

"Hello," Lloyd says after a moment. "You've reached the -"

He stops. I stay where I am, as my heart continues to pound in my chest. I don't even know why I'm so scared, but the last thing I want is to go down and interact with those two again. I'm worried that they might somehow draw me deeper into this mess, when all I want is to wait until the coast is clear, find my suitcase, and get the hell out of here.

"Who is it?" I hear the girl asking. A moment later, she asks again.

I hear the sound of a tinny voice coming from the phone. From up here, I can't make out any of the words, but I'm sure I remember that it's Matilda.

"Is she serious?" the girl continues. "Did she really go out there in this weather?"

As they continue to talk, I turn and crawl up the rest of the stairs, heading toward the landing. I still want to get out of this B&B, but I know for a fact that Lloyd and the girl are going to be loitering near the door for a while. Once I reach the top of the stairs, I stop and lean back against the wall. I can still hear muffled voices from downstairs, but I figure I have to wait a little longer before I can go back into the office and retrieve my things. Besides, I still have to locate my suitcase. I hadn't noticed until now, but I'm exhausted, probably because I haven't managed to sleep a wink since I arrived in this crazy place. I know I can't afford to sleep right now, but it's so tempting to lean my head back and close my eyes for a moment.

Which is when I hear the sobbing again.

I freeze, convinced that the sound has to be all in my head, but finally I open my eyes and realize that there really *is* someone weeping nearby. I look around at the various closed doors, trying to work out which room the sound is coming from, but it's not so easy to figure out the direction. After a moment, however, my eyes are drawn to the door in the far corner.

Room one.

Staring at the door, I realize that the crying

definitely seems to be coming from that room. I'm also starting to feel more and more certain that a child is responsible, maybe a little boy. I heard something similar earlier, while I was talking to Jude, but only for a few seconds. This time, the crying just keeps going on and on, until finally I get to my feet and take a couple of faltering steps toward the door.

By the time I get close enough to reach out for the handle, I'm *sure* that I've found the source of the crying sound.

I open my mouth to ask if everything is okay, but my throat feels impossibly dry.

"Hello?" I manage to gasp finally, although I doubt anyone heard me.

I wait.

Whoever's on the other side of this door, they sound grief-stricken.

"Hello?" I say again, knocking gently. "Are you... Are you okay?"

The sobbing continues.

I know that room one is occupied, because the key was missing from the hooks in the office, but I have no idea who's supposed to be staying in here.

"Hey," I continue, knocking again. "Do you want me to come in?"

I wait, but the sobbing continues.

"I'm coming in," I add, even though I'm not certain this is the best approach. I need to check all the rooms in case my suitcase has been hidden away, and besides, I can't just walk away when there's a child in trouble. "Okay? Just... I'm coming in to check on you."

I take a deep breath and then I turn the handle, only to find that the door is locked. I try again, still without any luck.

"Can you open up?" I ask, starting to worry that somehow in all this madness a little boy has become locked in one of the rooms. "Can you turn the latch? Are you alone in there?"

The sobbing continues, but this time I think I can just about hear the child trying to speak, as if he's mumbling something through his tears. I hold my breath, listening carefully, and I think maybe the boy is saying something about his father.

"Daddy," he whimpers, before his voice dissolves into more violent, retching sobs.

"Can you open the door for me?" I ask again, tapping gently. "I want to help you. Can you turn the latch on the inside?"

I wait.

"Can you hear me?" I continue. "Can -"

Suddenly, before I can get another word out, I hear an ear-piercing scream coming from outside the building. Stumbling back from the door, I pause for a moment before realizing I've heard that scream before. It takes another couple of seconds, though, before my racing mind is able to put everything together.

Matilda.

It was Matilda's scream, which means...

Hurrying over to the window, I look down at the yard just in time to see a figure stumbling out into the darkness. I recognize her immediately, of course. It's me, or the girl who looks like me at least, heading out into the snow.

"Where are you?" I hear her voice calling out, far below. "Matilda! Can -"

I watch as she stumbles, and as she then keeps going, frantically trying to get along the alley. I remember this moment so clearly, and I know that at any moment she's going to find the ketchup. There's a part of me that wants to slide the window up and warn her, to tell her that Matilda is just playing a stupid prank, but at the same time I can't help thinking that she looks pretty dumb stumbling about out there. Maybe she should learn her lesson the hard way. I watch as she disappears into the shadows, but then suddenly I hear a faint creaking sound over my shoulder.

Turning, I see to my shock that the door to room one has swung open.

CHAPTER EIGHT

"HELLO?" I CALL OUT cautiously, heading over to the door. "Is anyone in there?"

I can still hear the sobbing, although there's no sign of whoever's responsible, not even when I push the door all the way open and see the bed. The sound is definitely coming from somewhere in here, but so far the room looks to be completely empty. I take a step inside, and I'm immediately struck by the fact that this room feels much colder than any other room in the entire B&B. When I reach down and touch the radiator, I find that it's on full blast, but the heat seems to be making no difference to the rest of the room.

"Are you hiding?" I ask, looking toward the closet next to the window.

The sobbing continues, and I figure I should go take a look.

"I'm gonna open the doors, okay?" I continue, making my way around the bed and heading toward the closet. I grab the handles and hesitate for a moment, before pulling them open and finding nothing more than a set of suits hanging from the bar.

Crouching down, I double-check that there's nobody hiding anywhere inside, but all I discover at the bottom is a few pairs of shoes.

And now the sobbing sound definitely seems to be coming from somewhere over my shoulder. I turn and look at the bed, and I *swear* it sounds as if somebody is sitting there and weeping, but I still can't actually see anyone at all. I'm not given to flights of fancy but, after all the weirdness I've experienced so far tonight, the hairs on the back of my neck are definitely starting to sit up. Still, there's no sign of my suitcase in here, so I guess I should just go and keep searching.

Suddenly I lean down and look under the bed, convinced that I'll see whoever's sobbing.

Nothing. Just a few dust bunnies.

I sit up again, looking around the room. I'm starting to think that maybe this is all part of some very clever, very elaborate trick that's being played on me. It wouldn't be *that* difficult for somebody to hide some equipment in the room and play a recording, and I'm worried that I've accidentally become part of some twisted hidden-camera show. The last thing I need is to have my face broadcast, so I get to my feet, feeling as if this really *is* getting out of hand. I just need to find my goddamn suitcase and then never look back as I leave this B&B for good.

I step past the closet, but suddenly I hear the sound of a faint cry outside. Looking down at the alley,

I'm shocked to see what looks like a struggle. In a flash, I realize exactly what I'm witnessing. The girl is out there, and she's being attacked by some kind of dark, shadowy figure.

And she's looking at me.

For a moment, our eyes are fixed upon one another. She seems utterly shocked to see me, and I'm frozen to the spot as the sobbing continues behind me. All I can do is watch as the girl continues to fight back, and after a moment I squint, trying to get a better view of whoever or whatever is forcing her down. I can only really make out a faint shadow, however, although it seems to be keeping her in place with great ease.

Deep down, I'm almost impressed by its strength.

Deeper down, I'm horrified by that reaction.

And yet, that stupid girl got herself into this mess. She should never have gone rushing out into the snow, no when she knew full well that there's a killer on the loose. Besides, it's not like anything bad is going to happen to her. I know that she'll get away, that the attacker will suddenly pull back and leave her alone. I know that because I've lived through it already. And as I continue to watch her struggle, I feel a creeping realization start to move up through my chest.

She's me.

She's not some girl who *looks* like me.

She's really, truly me.

I can't even begin to explain what's happening here, or *how* it's happening. Maybe I'm just mad, maybe this is all a dream, maybe the world has gone completely off the rails, but I'm watching myself.

And sure enough, a moment later, the attacker pulls away, leaving the girl gasping in the snow.

She looks up at me again, and I can see the shock in her eyes, mixed with a little hatred. I remember that moment, I remember seeing the bandaged woman and wondering why she just stood and watched while I was being attacked. And now *I'm* the bandaged woman, watching as she stumbles through the snow and finally makes it back inside the building. I hear the door slamming shut, and then I reach up, touching the bandages that cover my face. My flesh no longer feels irritated, and when I slip my fingers beneath the bandages I find that the lotion seems to have dried up, which I guess means that perhaps it's done its job. I pull a section of the bandages away, then another section, until half my face is uncovered, and then I go to the mirror in the corner of the room.

My face looks a little sore still, but the worst of the rash has gone down. Carefully, I start pulling away the rest of the bandages, until finally they're all gone and I can see myself properly.

"Where's Daddy?" a little boy's voice asks suddenly.

Spinning around, I look over at the bed and see a boy sitting there, staring at me with tear-filled eyes.

"He's coming back, isn't he?" he continues, his bottom lip trembling slightly. "Tell me he's coming back. Tell me Mummy's wrong."

I stare at him, too shocked to react. He has neat, side-parted hair and he's wearing what looks like an old-fashioned school uniform, and I can see tears glistening as they trickle down his cheeks.

"I know he and Mummy have been sleeping in separate rooms lately," he whimpers, "but that's just because Daddy snores, isn't it? Daddy's coming back, he has to. If he doesn't, who will I play Onesies and Twosies with? I can't play by myself. And Mummy will clean the sheets. She's angry with me, she says I shouldn't have burst in there like that, but I was worried. And the sheets were so horrible. I don't like blood."

I open my mouth to reply, but no words come out.

A moment later, I hear bumping, stumbling steps somewhere else in the house, and I realize that somebody is coming up the stairs. It takes a moment before I realize what's happening, but then I hurry across the room and drop to my knees, peering through the keyhole just in time to see the earlier version of me disappearing into room four.

I freeze, too shocked to say anything, and a moment later she hauls her suitcase out.

"Thanks for nothing," she mutters under her breath, pausing for a moment and looking around, and then she starts dragging her suitcase down the stairs.

Suddenly I remember what happens next.

"Wait," I whisper, "watch out for the -"

I flinch as I hear her tripping and falling, and I know she just landed with her face in the plant. I can hear her scrambling to her feet, and I know that she's probably just starting to feel the first stings on her flesh. Too shocked to move, I listen as I hear her making her way down to the hallway. For a moment, all I can think about is what's going to happen to her next.

The office.

The lotion.

The knock on the door.

The sight of...

Wait, will that all really happen again?

"Are you going to look after me?" the little boy asks suddenly.

I turn to him. "What?"

He sniffs back more tears. "First it was Daddy," he continues, "and then it was Mummy. I don't like blood. I found Daddy, and then I found Mummy, but now have you come to find me? Are you going to look *after* me?"

"Look after you?" I hesitate for a moment, trying to figure out exactly what he means. "Are you here alone?" I ask finally. "Where are your parents?"

I wait, but he simply stares at me with dark, pain-filled eyes.

"Okay," I continue, "don't take this the wrong way, but you're kinda starting to freak me out. Are you staying here at the B&B alone, or are you with someone?"

"You look funny," he replies.

"Thanks," I mutter, before glancing over at the pile of bandages on the floor. I guess right about now, the other version of me is bandaging her face in the office, while yet another version is hauling her suitcase from the station, heading toward the front door. A moment later, as if to prove that fact, I hear someone knocking downstairs.

It's her.

I mean, it's me.

It's all about to start again.

"What are you scared of?" the little boy asks.

I turn to him. "Me? Why do you think I'm scared of something?"

"You look it."

I hear another knock downstairs.

"Yeah, well..." I pause for a moment, trying to figure out how the hell I'm going to get out of here. "You'd be looking a little ratty too," I add finally, "if you'd had the night I've had."

Heading to the window, I struggle with the latch for a moment before managing to pull it open. To be honest, I'm hoping to find a ladder or a roof I can use to climb out, but of course I don't have any such luck. As a strong wind howls through the window, I lean out and look down into the darkness, and then I look up and see several large chunks of ice hanging from the edge of the roof. Figuring that there's no way I can risk trying to climb down, I lean back and pull the window shut.

"What the hell am I going to do?" I whisper, trying to figure out when I can sneak downstairs and get out of here. The last thing I want is to run into *two* earlier versions of myself.

"Why do you think she did it?" the boy asks, sniffing back more tears.

I turn to him. "Huh?"

"Mummy said she'd look after me," he continues mournfully, "and then just a day later, she did exactly the same thing that he did. Why would she do that, when she told me she loved me?"

"I don't know what you're talking about," I tell him, heading over to take a closer look at his pale little face. Something about this kid is sending shivers through my chest, and I'm half-tempted to reach out and touch his shoulder, just to make sure he's really real. At the same time, I don't quite dare.

"The sheets were so white before," he tells me, "and then so red after. Redder than anything you can imagine. I still see them, even when I close my eyes. Watch."

He squeezes his eyes tight shut.

"I can see them!" he continues. "Right now!"

After a moment, he opens his eyes again.

"I thought they loved me," he stammers, "but they both did the same thing. They both made the sheets turn red, and now..." He pauses, and I swear I see a hint of anger simmering behind his eyes. "I hate them," he adds finally. "I hate them more than I ever hated anything else in my life. I hate them so much, I'd kill them if I could. I'd kill them all over again, every day! I hate them more than anyone ever hated anyone else in the whole world! And I'd make the sheets turn red again!"

"Who are you talking about?" I ask. "What -"

"I hate them!" he screams, suddenly lunging at me.

"Stop!" I stammer, stepping back. "You -"

Suddenly I see that the sheets beneath him are stained red, as if blood has began to soak through the cotton. For a moment, all I can do is stare in horror, but already blood is running down the sides of the bed and onto the carpet.

"I hate them!" the boy sneers, grabbing the sheets with his hands and pulling tight, forcing more blood to dribble between his fingers as he starts tearing the white fabric. "They ruined the sheets! They bled all over everything and they ruined it all! Look at the blood! These sheets were so clean before, but now -"

"You have a really nice place here," I hear a voice say suddenly, out on the landing.

Turning, I stare in horror at the door as I hear footsteps making their way past, along with the sound of a suitcase bumping against the floor.

"No," I whisper, "it can't be..."

"Thank you so much for letting me stay," the voice continues, in the distance now, as if they've entered one of the rooms.

"I have to get out of here," I stammer, finally feeling a horrific crushing sensation in my chest. I turn and look at the bed again, but suddenly the boy is gone and the sheets appear calm, unstained and undisturbed. Suddenly I'm filled with an intense, burning *need* to get the hell out of this place.

My fingers are trembling as I turn the latch, and I feel as if I might collapse as I pull the door open and peer out onto the landing. When I look over toward room four, I realize I can hear voices coming from inside, but the bandaged woman is turned partially away from me, which means...

Filled with panic, I creep across the landing and then scurry down the stairs, while taking care not to make any noise at all.

Once I'm down in the hallway, I feel a burst of relief as I scamper to the office door. When I go to grab my drying clothes from the chair, however, I'm shocked to see that they're gone.

"No," I whisper, looking around the room and realizing that there's still no sign of my suitcase. Then again, there's at least a *version* of my suitcase up in room four, but I can't go and get it unless I'm willing to encounter the two previous versions of myself. I hurry to the doorway and look toward the stairs, and for a moment I actually feel as if I might have the courage to just storm right up there.

Suddenly I hear footsteps coming down, and I panic. I hurry to the front door and pull it open, then I step outside and carefully pull the door shut, making sure to make almost no noise.

And now I'm locked out, shivering on the icy step, wearing nothing but a floral-patterned night-gown over my underwear. I pull the gown tight, but I'm already starting to feel the biting cold, and suddenly I realize that I might have made an absolutely massive mistake. I turn and try to push the door open, but of course it's locked now, so I take a step back and -

My right foot slips on the ice. I try to catch myself, but it's too late and I let out a gasp of shock as I fall back and land hard on the bottom step. Slithering down into the snow, I gasp again as I feel a thumping pain in my shoulder, and for a few seconds all I can manage is to stay right here on the ground as more snows falls on me.

Staring up at the dark night sky, with snow drifting down, I feel for a moment as if maybe I should just stay right here. Eventually the snow would cover me completely.

Finally, worried that I'm going to freeze to death if I stay out here, I stumble to my feet. There's no point trying to go back through the front door, so I limp around through the snow and make my way to the alley at the rear of the building. The last thing I want to do is venture into the darkness, especially when I know that there was someone out here a little earlier, but I'm freezing to death and I figure I have no choice. I push my way through the snow, forcing myself onward until I reach the yard, and then I try the door to the boiler room, only to find that it's locked.

"Damn you!" I hiss, trying it a couple more times before stepping back and then trying to push it open with my shoulder. I try again, causing the door to shudder in its frame, but there's clearly no way I'm going to force my way inside. I'm a little out of breath now, so I take a step back and try to come up with another plan.

"Help me," I whimper, before realizing that nobody's going to be able to hear me. "Come on, please, give me a break."

I have to do something.

Filled with a sudden sense of determination, I realize that there's no longer any point hiding from what's happening. I need to face this thing head-on, the way I should have done in the first place. Feeling colder and colder, I start stomping back through the snow, making my way along the alley and out onto the street again. I'm going to go right up to the front door of the B&B and I'm going to knock, and then I'm going to go inside and confront both the previous versions of myself and I'm going to tell them what's happening. Then I'm going to get dressed, get my suitcase down from the room, and not let anything stop me as I head straight out the door again.

I mean, sure, I don't remember that happening the first time around, or the second, but I don't care. This time, nothing is going to stop me.

Struggling through the snow, I finally get to the front of the building. I have to tread carefully, since there's a hell of a lot of ice, but eventually I make it all the way to the foot of the steps.

Suddenly spotting a hint of movement, I look up at the office window. To my surprise, I see Lloyd holding the net curtains open and staring out at the street. After just a moment, he looks straight down at me and our eyes meet.

I remember this moment.

Sort of, anyway. I remember being in the office, with my face bandaged, and finding Lloyd at the window. And I remember him saying that he'd seen someone rushing past the B&B, except...

As I stare at him, I realize that he's watching me with a freakishly calm expression. I want to look away, I want to go and knock on the door, but I can feel a sense of fear rising through my chest, threatening to numb me completely. No matter how much I try to tell myself that I'm over-reacting, the fear grows and grows, reaching up with long, thin fingers that seem to be wriggling through my neck and up toward the base of my skull.

I take a step back through the snow, watching as his lips start to move, but the sense of fear is still getting stronger. I let out a faint whimper, and suddenly I realize that the entire B&B seems to be radiating an overwhelming sense of death. I don't know how I never noticed it before, but the building itself is silently screaming at me, telling me to get the hell away, and a moment later I realize I can see two faces behind Lloyd. My first assumption is that one of them has to be the bandaged version of me, but instead I see that Jude is standing over his left shoulder, and her dead husband Herb is on the other side, and all three of them are watching me with cold, dark eyes. Behind them, on the far side of the room, the bandaged version of me is just entering.

I remember that moment, but I didn't see Jude or Herb. I only saw Lloyd. But now...

Suddenly Lloyd taps on the glass and smiles. In an instant, I realize that I recognize his face from somewhere else. He's the boy who was on the bed upstairs, in room one. Which means Jude and Herb are, or were, his parents.

The sense of fear is growing, overwhelming, until finally I can't help myself.

Unable to help myself, I turn and start racing along the street, scrambling desperately through the snow despite the pain in my legs. Never before in my life have I felt such a pure sense of fear, and it's as if some deeper, more basic instinct has taken complete control of my body, pushing my mind aside and forcing me into survival mode. The snow is deep and heavy, but all I can think about is the fact that I have to get as far away from the B&B – and from Lloyd – as possible, and then I have to make sure I never, ever go back. Gasping as I feel my legs starting to burn with the effort of wading through so much snow, I nevertheless keep going until I reach the very end of the street, and then I run along the next street and the next, racing through the maze of narrow, winding medieval roads until suddenly my legs buckle and I drop down into the snow, panting and desperately gasping for air.

I can still feel the fear, but it's not nearly as strong now.

Turning, I look back along the snowy street, and I swear I can sense the B&B's evil throbbing in the night air. How am I the only one? How are all the other people in Canterbury not aware of this? And how did I not notice until now?

"There!" I remember Lloyd saying earlier, when he tapped the office window while I was in the room. "I saw someone!"

He claimed he saw someone skulking through the shadows, but now I know he was lying. He must have realized it was me outside, so why didn't he admit that? And why, at the time, did I not see Jude and Herb standing next to him?

My legs are stinging, but I slowly get to my feet and start brushing clumps of snow from my soaking night-gown. I'm cold, but at least the effort of running has warmed me up a little. Still, when I try pulling the night-gown tighter for a little warmth, I find that it's cold and wet. If I don't find something else to wear soon, I think I might actually die.

My first instinct is to go back to the train station. I can wait there all night, if necessary, and catch the next train to London. The idea seems pretty perfect, until suddenly I realize that all my possessions and all my money are in the suitcase and my jacket pocket, back at the hotel. I check the pockets of the night-gown, but I don't have so much as a penny. After all my careful work, and all my planning, I've lost everything. I can't go home without the suitcase. I need the money, so I can give it back to the people I stole it from. So I can begin to make amends.

"Come on," I whisper, shaking my head, convinced that there has to be some way out of this mess. "Think, Bobbie," I continue, trying to give myself a pep-talk as I start shivering violently in the cold. "You can do this. You can just go back to the B&B and make them give you your stuff..."

My voice trails off as I realize that there's no way I can do that.

I can't *ever* go to the B&B again, not when I felt such a powerful sense of evil. I can even feel the evil now, although it's much weaker since I'm several blocks away. Something about the sight of Lloyd in that window seems to have driven pure dread into my chest. I'll never be brave enough to go back, not now.

As I start limping through the darkness, past unlit shop windows, I feel all manner of pains making their presence known throughout my body. My arms, my ankles, my hips, my chest... I've taken such a battering tonight, I feel as if I might be about to collapse.

And finally that's exactly what happens, just as I reach the next corner. Dropping to my knees, I feel a swelling surge of pain under my rib-cage. That's one part of me that I actually *don't* remember hurting tonight, but it pains me anyway for a few more seconds before passing. Then I'm left still on my knees, trying to find the strength to stand, knowing that if I fall again I might never get up.

In the distance, there are faint bells. Or maybe not bells, maybe glasses clinking together.

I turn and look, and to my surprise I see that there are several bright, warm lights moving inside an otherwise dark restaurant over on the far side of the cobbled square. I stare for a moment, convinced that I must be hallucinating, that these overgrown fireflies can't possibly be real, but then I see one of them being set down on a table and I realize that they must be lanterns.

Lanterns carried by men.

The sight is totally bizarre, like something out of an old Christmas card, but it's enough to get me back up on my feet. I should edge around the sides of the square, using the windows as support, but instead I push out into the snow, crossing past the war memorial as I stagger toward the restaurant. I can see my own reflection in the glass, but I can also see the faces of men talking as they carry their lanterns about, and finally one of them glances this way and sees me.

I stumble and fall, landing hard on my knees. Just as I start to get up, however, I hear a door creaking open. A moment later, someone takes my arm.

"Let me help you there," he says, supporting my weight as I stumble to my feet. "You're freezing. Come inside, we've got lamps that'll warm you."

Limping along with him, I let him lead me into the restaurant, where half a dozen other men are buttoning their dark uniforms shut, as if they're preparing to head outside. At first, I mistake them for police officers, but I quickly realize that they actually seem to be civilians, although I can't make out their faces properly. No matter what part of the darkened room they're in, their faces seem to be perpetually shadowed.

"I'll catch up to you," the man next to me says, turning to the others. "I just need to make sure this young lady's alright first. Go on ahead, and remember to be vigilant. He'll be on the prowl tonight, there's no doubt about it."

I look over at him, but his face is shadowed too. I can see the faintest hint of his features, but nothing more.

As the rest of the men file out, holding lanterns that somehow light their way without lighting their faces, I stumble toward a lamp that's burning on one of the restaurant's tables. As soon as I hold my hands closer, I feel a rush of desperately-needed warmth. Turning, I look out the windows just in time to see several silhouettes trampling away through the snow, spreading out and heading down various side-streets. It takes a moment before I realize that the man who found me is now over on the far side of the room, retrieving something from beneath the counter.

"Now what were you doing out there, eh?" he asks. "Freezing to death, I shouldn't wonder. It's not the kind of night to be out alone, you know. Even if there wasn't the Snowman to worry about, you're still in danger of catching hypothermia."

He comes over to me and sets a pile of dark clothes on the table. I tilt my head, still trying to see his face properly, but again there are too many shadows. The room might be dark, but I'm sure the lantern on the nearby table should be casting at least *some* light across his features.

"These are on the house," he continues. "You need to change out of what you're in."

Gratefully taking the clothes, I look around for somewhere I can change.

"I can turn my back," the man says, turning away from me. "Don't worry, I won't look. Or you can go into the storeroom at the back. We use this restaurant as a kind of staging post whenever we have to go out at night."

I hesitate, before realizing that I don't really have much choice. I start peeling the wet gown away from my flesh, although in several places the freezing fabric has started sticking to my body.

"Do you have somewhere to stay tonight?" the man asks after a moment. "We're a volunteer night-watch group. We walk the streets on nights like this, hoping to keep the city safe. The police do what they can, but we like to think we help a little. Of course, with this Snowman character rumored to be out and about again, we're taking extra precautions tonight. We might just look like a bunch of do-gooder old codgers, but we're all ex-servicemen, so we know a thing or two about taking care of ourselves."

"I'm okay," I stammer, setting the gown on the table. My underwear is soaked too, so I double-check that the man is looking away and then I strip down. Grabbing the dry clothes, I quickly start slipping into them, and I find that he's found me one of their uniforms. It's not exactly a look I've ever tried before, but it's warm and dry and I'm so grateful.

"Are you a runaway?" he asks.

"No," I reply. "Not really."

"So where's home?"

"A long way away."

"But tonight, I mean. You didn't look like you were dressed to be out just now."

"I was staying at the..." My voice trails off as I finish getting dressed. I guess there's no harm in telling the old man where I've been. "I'm done now. It's okay, you can turn around. I was staying at the Castle Crown B&B. Maybe you -"

Suddenly I hear a faint gasp coming from his lips, as if he's shocked.

"The Castle Crown B&B," I say again, in case he misheard. "It's not far from here, it's just -"

"I know where it is," he replies, interrupting me. "What in the name of all that's holy were you doing there?"

"Long story," I mutter. "Why? Do you know the place?"

"Everyone knows the Castle Crown," he tells me, turning this way but keeping his face in the shadows. "They might not want to talk about it, but they sure know the stories."

He hesitates for a moment, before stepping closer and reaching a hand out toward my arm. Still, his face is hidden in the room's shadows, as if the lantern's flickering light isn't picking out his features at all.

"Do you mind if I check something?" he asks.

"What?"

"Humor me."

He hesitates, before touching my arm, holding it for a moment as if he can't quite believe what he's feeling.

"Well, stone the crows," he continues finally, sounding a little relieved. "It's been a long, long time since a live 'un managed to make it out of that place."

CHAPTER NINE

"Castle Crown has been in the same family for years," the old man explains as he pours us a cup of tea each. "I don't know how far back exactly, but when I moved to the area it was owned by Herb and Jude Landon."

"Herb and Jude?" I ask, immediately thinking back to the strange couple I met earlier tonight.

"Nice people," he continues, sliding a cup of tea along the counter toward me. "Friendly. Open to strangers. Definitely not the kind you'd ever expect to be hiding something. I knew Herb quite well, and I never guessed he was sick, not until one day we got a call to say he'd been found dead. The poor guy was dying, and he didn't want to put his wife through any more misery. He waited 'til she was out for the day, and then he cut his wrists in the bath."

"What are you talking about?" I reply, trying not to panic. "I just -"

I catch myself just in time. The last thing I want

is to start ranting about ghosts. At the same time, I can't help thinking back to the sight of Lloyd standing in the office window, flanked by those two figures. I could see them when I was outside, but not when I was actually in the room.

"Could you do me a favor?" I ask. "I know this is kind of a big one, but could you go to the B&B for me and fetch my suitcase?"

"Your *what*?"

"It's really important. It's kinda life or death, actually."

He immediately shakes his head. I might not be able to see his features, but he's silhouetted against the restaurant's window as snow falls outside.

"Please," I continue. "I can even pay you. I just -"

"I'm not going there," he says firmly. "You'll not find many who are willing, not these days, not since *he* took over."

"Who?" I ask cautiously.

"After Herb killed himself, it was their son who found the body. Just a little kid, no more than eight or nine years old. I can't even begin to imagine what that does to a child, but there was more to come. The next day, overcome by grief I suppose, Herb's widow Jude took the same way out. She cut her wrists on the bed, and do you wanna guess who found her? That poor kid. One parent one day, the other the next. If he wasn't damaged in the head from Herb, he sure as well after he found his mother."

"A little boy?" I whisper, thinking back to the

child I met in one of the rooms this evening. "What happened to him after his parents died?"

"What *happened* to him?" the man replies, sounding concerned by the question. "Nothing much, at least not from the outside. He grew up and took over the Castle Crown B&B, and he still runs it to this day. He's a weird chap, and no mistake. I've never much cared for him, but maybe I'm just showing my prejudice there. Hell, there's probably nothing wrong with poor old Lloyd. In fact, given the cards he was dealt as a boy, it's a wonder he turned out as well as he did. Of course, I haven't seen him in years. I don't think many have."

"Lloyd?" I stammer, thinking back to the polite, mild-mannered man I met at the B&B. "Lloyd runs the Castle Crown?"

"Not that he gets many guests these days. He doesn't even advertise. Just a business card here and there. How did *you* find the place?"

"I called around," I tell him. "I tried all the B&B numbers I could find, but they were all fully-booked for the night. Then I found a card for the Castle Crown on the floor of the phone-box, and I figured it was worth a shot."

"Well, I wouldn't go back there, not if I were you," he explains. "He's a strange chap, and no mistake. When were you due to go home, anyway?"

"Home?"

The word sends a shiver through my chest. For a moment, I try to imagine what it would be like if I walk through the door and tell them I don't have their money. No matter how much I apologize, they'll hate me, and they'll have every justification. They took me in a long time ago, they treated me as a family, and I betrayed them. I stole. All the apologies in the world won't mean anything, not if I've lost the money. If I go back empty-handed, I can't even begin to make things right.

"What happened?" the old man asks suddenly.

I turn to him.

"I can see it in your eyes," he continues, with a faint smile. "You *are* running away from something."

"So?"

"So nobody can run forever."

"*I* can!" I tell him defiantly. "It's not like they'd want to see me again anyway. If I go home, they'll just..."

My voice trails off, and after a moment I close my eyes and imagine the hatred I'll have to see in their eyes if I *do* go home. The shock. The sense of betrayal. I deserve all of that and more. I deserve to go to jail. I'm an awful person.

"I did something bad," I whisper finally.

"I'm sure it wasn't as -"

"Really bad," I add, turning to him. "So bad that I can't ever go home."

"And what might your crime have been?"

I open my mouth, poised to tell him that I can't reveal the truth, but suddenly I feel as if I really need to get it off my chest. I look around the dark, deserted restaurant, and then I turn back to him.

"I deserve everything that's happened to me tonight," I say finally, "and more. I deserve it because I stole something, and because I ran away like a coward.

And then I lost the only thing I can use to make it up to them."

It takes a long time for me to tell him the whole story. Partly because a lot happened, but also partly because I take a meandering path through the facts, constantly stopping and backing-up a little, trying to put everything in context. There are things I don't want to tell him, parts of the story that I still don't want to admit, but I force myself through these little roadblocks. After all, it's not the kind of story that can be half-told. Finally, feeling a flash of relief, I get to the end and fall silent.

I wait for him to say something, but he's simply sitting calmly by the window, as if he thinks I have more to tell him.

"I'm a bad person," I say after a moment. "See? I told you."

He pauses, before taking a sip of tea.

"And I can't go home," I continue. "Not ever."

"That's not entirely true," he replies. "You *can* go home."

"I'll be arrested!"

"Probably."

"And I lost the money!"

"Apparently so."

"And they'll..." I take a deep breath, trying to stay calm. "They'll hate me. If I had the money, I could go back and give it to them, and I could try to make things right. But without the money, all I have is words and apologies, and that's not what they need."

"You can't be sure that they hate you."

"Of course they do. I did something terrible."

He pauses, and then he starts slowly nodding.

"I'm a bad person," I continue. "No-one who's good would do something like that. They took me in after my own parents died, they raised me and loved me for a decade. And I repaid them by lying and stealing, and then I ran away from the mess I'd created."

"You certainly seem to have made some bad choices," he mutters.

"They don't want to see me," I point out, with tears in my eyes. "They're probably sick of the sight of me. And they'd be at the trial, they'd watch me as I was sent to jail."

"I'm no expert," he replies, "but the amount you took, and the way you did it... It's certainly possible that you might have to serve some time behind bars. Especially since you ran away. I don't think the courts look too kindly on that type of thing, not when you take advantage of somebody's trust."

"It was so easy," I whisper, thinking back to the day when I first came up with the plan. "It was easy because they treated me like family. I know there's no excuse, I know nothing justifies it. I just... I'd never seen so much money in my life, and then one day it was just sitting there in the open, waiting for them to take it to the bank. I had this moment of weakness, and by the time I realized what I'd done, it was too late. If I could go back and undo it, I would, but I can't."

"You could get the money back and give it to them," he suggests. "They might decide to help you."

I shake my head, and now there are tears in my eyes.

"They might," he continues.

"Of course they wouldn't! I'm a bad person and they hate me!"

"But taking the money back would be the right thing to do," he points out. "You're not a bad person, not if you accept responsibility for what you did and face the consequences."

I shake my head.

"Why not?"

"Because I'm too scared!" I hiss, wiping tears from my cheeks. "Anyway, I don't even have the money, not anymore. It's back at the B&B."

"I can see how that's a problem."

"I'm a criminal," I continue, leaning forward as I feel a wave of shock run through my chest. "For the rest of my life, I have to live with the knowledge that when the easy option was presented to me, I took it. I lied and I cheated. Apparently that's the kind of person I am."

"You can change the kind of person you are."

I shake my head.

In the distance, the bells of a church ring out across the city. They seem faraway and close at the same time, as if the freezing night air is thinning the sound.

"I have to get out on patrol," the man says with a sigh, standing and heading toward the door. "I can't leave the other members of the night-watch short-handed for too long. There are a lot of streets in this fair city, and we need to cover as many of them as possible. You're welcome to come with me, but I'd much rather you go find yourself somewhere safe to stay for the rest of the night and then head home in the morning. Failing that, you can at least stay here tonight. It's not safe to be out on the streets."

"I'm fine," I tell him, getting to my feet and limping over to join him as he pulls the door open. "Thank you for the dry clothes, though. I'll return them."

"No need."

"I will, though," I continue, stepping back out into the cold, snowy night air. "As soon as I can, I'll get them washed and I'll bring them back."

"I'd rather you go home."

I shake my head.

"You can't assume that those people hate you," he tells me. "Give them a chance. The alternative is trying to run forever, and that'll never work."

"I can't go home," I reply. "Not without their money."

"Are you sure you don't want to stay here in the warm, at least for a few more hours?"

"I need to keep going," I tell him, turning and looking across the snow-covered square. "I'll figure something out. I always do."

"And look where that got you."

I take a couple of steps back. "Good luck with your patrol," I tell him. "Maybe you'll be lucky and the Snowman won't strike tonight."

"He always strikes when there's snow falling," he replies, still holding the restaurant's door open. "People huddle safe in their houses, but there's always someone who makes a mistake and braves the elements. That's why I don't want you being out here alone like this. Won't you *please* consider accepting my offer? Stay in the restaurant, just until morning. That way, I'll know you're safe."

"I can look after myself," I reply. "I'm probably not even the Snowman's type, anyway. Don't worry, if I hear anyone nearby, I'll run."

"No, I insist," he continues, placing a hand on my arm. He leans closer, and finally I can just about make out his fearful eyes. "A girl out alone in this weather? I lost my own daughter Elizabeth to this monster, many years ago. You'll never -"

And then he's gone. I stare at the spot where he was standing, but there's no sign of him. A moment later, I realize I can still feel his hand on my arm, but the sensation quickly fades.

"Hello?" I call out, turning and looking around.

No reply.

I look back toward the shuttered restaurant. There are no lights inside at all now, and it's hard to believe I was ever in there. Still, I'm wearing the dry uniform, so I know I didn't imagine the whole thing.

"Hello?" I shout again, before realizing that I'm all alone.

Turning, I head along the street, pushing through the snow. I glance over my shoulder several times, just in case the man reappears, but there's still no sign of him. Finally reaching the street corner, I turn and look around, but there's no sign of the old man, or of anyone else. In fact, right now I feel as if I'm the only person in the entire city. I don't even see the men with lanterns.

I pick a street at random, making my way along a curved pavement that runs close to the cathedral gate.

I've been like this before, I've been desperate, and I've always come up with a plan. There's just something about my brain that means I can't think properly until my back's against the wall. If I'm comfortable and safe, I just let myself float along. But if I'm in trouble, or in danger, some extra gear clicks into action and I start figuring out what to do. And now, as I make my way along another street, I can feel the fear creeping through my chest. If I keep on like this, wandering alone, I'll end up as some homeless wretch dying on the street. I have to come up with a plan.

And then I stop, seeing a familiar shape on the ground just a few meters away. Stepping closer, I reach down and carefully take hold of the book, lifting it from the pure white snow. Even before I've turned it around to look at the front cover, I know the title.

"*The Wind in the Willows*," I read out loud, shuddering as I realize that Matilda must have dropped her book earlier when she ran from the B&B.

I guess that's the part of the night's events I've reached now. She must be out here somewhere.

Snow is falling all around me as I shove the book into my jacket pocket. The entrance to the cathedral precinct is unlocked, so I slip through, forcing my way through the snow. As soon as I'm on the other side, I see a payphone over by the wall, with the handset hanging down at the side. I wade over, and now I can hear a faint voice on the other end of the line, saying Matilda's name over and over.

It's Lloyd.

Lifting the receiver, I listen to him calling

Matilda's name a few more times. He sounds worried.

"It's me," I say finally.

He pauses. "Bobbie?"

"Yeah," I continue with a faint smile, realizing that as far as he's concerned, I probably just left the building a short while ago. "Have you... Have you called the police yet?"

"I thought I should keep the line open," he stammers. "Is there any sign of her?"

I turn and look across the precinct, toward the huge, magnificent cathedral that towers above me just a couple of hundred feet away.

"Not so far," I reply, before looking down and seeing footprints all around me in the snow. For a moment, I try to figure out which way they lead, but I quickly realize that they criss-cross each other with such frequency that it's impossible to pick out a path. "She was definitely here, though. I found her book on the ground."

"You really shouldn't be out there," he continues, sounding increasingly worried. "Please, won't you come back at once?"

He sounds as if he actually cares.

"She'll be fine," I tell him.

"And how do you know that?"

"Trust me," I continue. "I just do. She'll be back at the B&B real soon."

"Well, I suppose. That's a relief, at least."

"I didn't know you owned the place," I continue. "You never mentioned that."

I wait, but he doesn't reply.

"Lloyd?"

Silence. The line is still open, but it's as if he's suddenly fallen silent.

"I know about your parents," I tell him, feeling a growing sense of fear in my chest. "I know that the little boy in room one is you, but you're not dead, are you? But the boy is definitely you, and I saw the way he gripped those bloodied sheets, and I heard his voice and I -"

Suddenly the call ends.

"Lloyd?"

I guess maybe I was boring him. That, or he just thinks I'm insane.

Or he knows I'm onto him.

"You're the Snowman," I whisper, feeling a shudder pass up my spine. I don't have it all figured out yet, but I'm sure I'm right. "You're the Snowman," I say again. "You killed those people."

After putting the phone back on the hook, I start wading through the snow, following the line of prints that leads around the cathedral's southern side. My progress is painfully slow and my legs are already aching, while my thin jacket is providing little protection from the snow and has instead begun to feel unpleasantly damp. I never knew I was quite so out of shape, but by the time I make it to the edge of the cathedral, I'm actually short of breath, and I have to stop for a moment to regather my composure. Looking around, I see that the snow has been disturbed in several directions, which means -

"He's not out here, dummy," Matilda says

suddenly.

Startled, I turn and find her standing right behind me, staring at me with dark, pain-filled eyes.

"I found your book," I tell her, taking the copy of *The Wind in the Willows* from my pocket. "I guess you..."

My voice trails off as I see that there's a trickle of blood running from the corner of her mouth.

"Are you okay?" I ask cautiously. "Matilda?"

"He's not out here," she continues. "They're looking in the wrong place. They always have been. He never kills in the street. Why would he? He's not a fool. The last thing he wants is to get caught out here, bent over his latest victim. He kills them at home. He just brings them outside to dump their bodies."

"What are you talking about?" I stammer, taking a step back.

"It's pretty easy, really," she says, starting to smile. "The only hard part is luring them inside, but even that can be done when you have a reason for perfect strangers to enter your house. He doesn't have to trick them or anything like that. He just has to wait, and he knows that when the weather is bad, even the most neglected, most ignored guesthouse is going to get a customer or two. Some poor little stranded waif will knock on the door and ask if he has rooms, and they'll be so glad when he nods, they'll practically fall over themselves to get inside."

"Who will?" I ask, even though I'm starting to think I can guess. "Matilda..."

"He kills us in our rooms," she continues,

holding her arms up to reveal the bloody slits on her wrists. "On the nice fresh, crisp white sheets. Just like his parents. Sure, he leaves the bodies out in the snow once he's done with them. He left *me* near the train station. That was a *long* time ago, though. It's hard to keep track for sure, but I think it's many years since the night *I* showed up. I was just like you, though. Lost and alone, in need of a bed for the night. Can you imagine how he must have felt when I showed up? He must have been licking his lips in anticipation."

I watch with a growing sense of horror as blood dribbles from her torn wrists and spatters against the snow.

"You'll be like the rest of us soon," she says, stepping toward me. "Once he's added you to his collection."

"I'm not going back," I stammer, realizing that she means Lloyd. "No way. I'm never going there again."

"Oh, silly," she replies, grinning broadly. "You're *already* there, remember?"

"But -"

"And you just spoke to him on the phone. He's gonna know that you know. Now you just have to wait and see when he decides to make you scream. It's too late to stop him. You're already bound to the place."

"I'm not going back," I stammer.

She laughs. "You've already been back."

"Of course I haven't!"

"Yes you have. You can't fight it." She steps closer still, until I can see her pale, bloodless face in the moonlight. "You can't undo something that's already happened to you."

I shake my head, before turning and running, racing through the snow. I slip several times, crashing down, but I keep getting back up and rushing through the streets. I don't even know where I'm going, all I know is that I have to get as far from this city as possible. And then, with no warning, I run out from a side-street and slip, crashing to a halt in the snow and finding myself staring up at the impossible sight of the Castle Crown B&B towering above me.

Realizing that I accidentally ran all the way back here, I scramble to my feet and race along the street, heading toward the train station. As soon as I run around the next corner, however, I stop suddenly as I see that once again I'm right in front of the B&B.

"That's not possible," I stammer, taking a step back. "No way!"

I turn and run again, this time heading in the other direction, determined to get away. Somehow the snow feels thicker and harder to get through, but I keep pushing as I make my way along a pitch-black street. Glancing over my shoulder, I make double-sure that I can see the B&B far behind me, and then I turn and keep going, struggling toward the end of the street, determined to find my way out of this city. I almost fall several times, but pure fear keeps me going until I finally spill out at the crossroads and look around, trying to figure out which way to go next.

I freeze as soon as I see that I'm once again in front of the B&B.

"What's wrong with you?" I gasp, convinced that this time I can't have made a mistake. "You won't let me go, is that it? Well -"

I catch myself just in time, just before I tell an inanimate building to go to hell. Still, I mutter a few curses under my breath as I turn and take a different side-street, past several shuttered shops. I cross the road, and after a moment I look back. Sure enough, I can see the rear of the B&B in the distance.

"It's behind me," I whisper, trying to fix whatever's wrong in my head. "It's definitely behind me."

With that, I turn and push through the snow, heading toward the next corner. I should come out somewhere near the supermarket car park, but my knees are aching and my ankle is sending ripples of pain up my leg. I keep pushing, fighting through each and every stumble, until I collapse against a bollard. For a few seconds, I feel a fresh, simmering pain in my chest, and I can barely even get breath into my lungs. Finally, however, I realize I can feel a familiar sense of dread creeping over my shoulders. Even before I lift my head, I know what I'm going to see.

"How is that possible?" I whisper.

The B&B is right in front of me, towering high into the night sky. Snow is falling all around, rustling gently as it lands.

"I can't run?" I continue, forcing myself up from the bollard and taking a step back. "Is that it? You're trying to show me I can't run?"

I wait, and for a moment I swear I'm almost

expecting an answer. Maybe I'm getting delirious, or maybe the events of this endless night have begun to wear me down, but either way the building remains firmly and resolutely in front of me.

"I'm not going back inside," I stammer, with tears in my eyes. "You can't make me."

Turning, I start limping through the snow. Maybe running was a mistake, maybe running allowed me to become confused by the snaking, winding streets of this old city. But walking away, calmly and slowly, is a different matter entirely. I look over my shoulder and see the B&B getting further and further away with each step, and then I look ahead and keep walking. A harsh wind has begun to pick up now, blowing snow against me as if the elements are trying to force me back, but I won't let anything stop me. I let out a few pained grunts as I stumble onward, and I have to stop and lean against a couple of bollards, but finally I get to the next corner.

So far, so good.

I look back again, and the B&B is barely visible in the haze of snow.

Satisfied that maybe I'm finally getting away, I turn and limp along the next street. I'm freezing, and even the uniform I was given by the old man is starting to fail me as I feel the cold wind blowing through the fibers. My ankle is throbbing now, as if the myriad slips and bumps are finally making their combined presence felt, and I want nothing more than to just stop and rest for a moment. But I know that if I let my guard down, if I even close my eyes or let my mind drift, I'll find myself right back in front of the B&B.

When I get to the next corner, I find myself outside a pub. There are no lights on, of course, but I stop for a moment and lean against the wall. I don't dare close my eyes, I don't dare think about anything else. I simply focus on the fact that the B&B is now several blocks away, and then I start walking again. I know I'm close to city wall, and I can see the lights of Canterbury East train station in the distance. If I can just make it to the platform, I can sit on one of the benches and wait for the first train to arrive in the morning. I'll sneak on-board without a ticket, and I'll go to London, and I'll disappear into the crowds and somehow I'll find a way to survive.

Somehow I'll -

Suddenly my ankle buckles. I let out a gasp as I fall, but at the last moment I manage to grab a bollard and hold myself up. The pain is intense, and I squeeze my eyes tight shut as I wait for the worst to subside.

And before I even open them again, I know what I'll find.

Looking up, I see the B&B once again towering above me.

Letting out a gasp of anger, I turn and run. My ankle is agony, but I don't stop, not even when I reach the end of the next street and find myself in front of the B&B yet again. Turning and running again, I slip through street after street, and sure enough I keep coming back to the B&B. Refusing to accept this as my fate, I push on through the night, trying every possible twist and turn through the city streets but always, always ending up at the same spot. I won't give in, though, so I keep going despite the growing pain in my chest. I slip several times, but I force myself onward and onward, running past the B&B over and over again until finally I try hurrying down the alley at the rear.

Suddenly I slam into a figure in the dark. We both fall to the ground, and I'm about to apologize when I see the figure's face.

It's me.

She struggles to get free, but I hold her down. No matter how hard she tries to get back up, pure panic compels me to keep her under me. At least she can't see my face, not in the darkness. I briefly consider warning her, but somehow the words won't leave my mouth. I'm not quite sure why she's out there, but suddenly I spot movement in one of the nearby windows, and I look up just in time to see the bandaged woman standing in the window, watching us.

Watching both of us.

For a moment, three versions of me are staring at each other. Filled with a sudden sense of fear, I finally clamber off the version on the ground and run away into the darkness, desperate to get as far from this hellish place as possible. I hurry along the next street, gasping for breath, before finally dropping to my knees in the snow. I take a few seconds to get air back into my lungs, and then I raise my head and look up at the inevitable sight before me.

"I can't get away," I whisper, feeling a flood of resignation in my chest as I look at the front of the B&B. "You won't let me, will you?"

I stare at the door for a moment, before spotting something glinting in the snow. Staggering forward, I reach down and find a set of keys frozen in the snow. It takes a few seconds for me to dig around the edges, but finally I pull the keys out and see that they're attached to a plastic fob.

Room four.

These are the keys I was given when I first arrived. The keys I was somehow given by another version of myself. I guess I must have dropped them on one of the many occasions I slipped on the icy steps at the front of the building. I stare down at them for a moment as they rest in my hands, and slowly I start to realize that there's no way I'm ever going to get away. I can run all night, but the night will never end, not until I surrender. I can't beat those odds. I have to go back inside and find my suitcase.

Grabbing the railing, I carefully make my way up the steps, taking care not to slip on the ice. My hand is trembling as I slip the key into the door, and then I hesitate for a moment before pushing it open.

Ahead, the dark hallway seems to be waiting for me. Despite the immense pain in my ankle, I limp back inside.

CHAPTER TEN

EVERYTHING IS CALM. QUIET. Peaceful. I don't hear any voices, or any struggles, or any footsteps on the stairs. It's almost as if the entire B&B has suddenly put its toys away and begun to hold its breath.

Limping along the hallway, I reach the door to the office and look through. My clothes aren't on the chair, and the metal poker is still leaning against the wall. I've completely lost track of what point I've reached in this endless, repeating night, but evidently I'm not yet at the point where my earlier self comes rushing through to dry her clothes and to wrap lotion and bandages around her face. That part of the madness is yet to come.

A moment later I hear a bump below, and I look down at the floorboards. Maybe an earlier version of me is in the boiler room right now, or maybe I'm in the breakfast room. Maybe I'm also upstairs in one of the rooms, perhaps talking to the strange little boy who one

171

day grew up to be Lloyd. Maybe I'm in all those places at once. No matter how hard I try to keep the whole thing straight in my head, I still can't quite make sense of it all, and I finally realize that I don't even need to try. Besides, the edges of the various incidents probably don't even match up perfectly.

I'm not here to understand.

I'm here to get the suitcase, and to leave the B&B, and then I have to go to the train station. And then... Despite the fear in my chest, I know that I won't be taking the train to London. I won't be trying to survive on a bundle of cash that would inevitably run out one day anyway. I'll be going home, and I'll be giving the money back, and I'll be facing up to whatever punishment awaits me.

I'm finally going to do the right thing.

First, though, I need to figure out where I left the suitcase. If it's not in the office, I guess the most likely place is room four. Rather than stopping to untangle all the conflicting threads, I start limping up the stairs. If I run into people, then I run into them, although I guess I'd remember if that had happened earlier. Sure enough, when I get to the landing, there's no sign of anyone, although a moment later I hear a very faint creak on the next flight of stairs.

I look over just in time to see the timid woman creeping down, but once again she stops as soon as she sees me, and then she slowly starts backing up again.

"Wait!" I hiss, stepping over to her, but she's already gone.

I look up the stairs for a moment, feeling a shiver

pass through my chest.

"Who are you?" I whisper, hoping that she might come back. "Are you Betty? Are you Elizabeth?"

I wait, but finally I realize I have to keep moving. Some mysteries just have to remain mysteries forever. Turning, I head over to room four and unlock the door, and then I slip inside. The room is empty, with the neat bed still undisturbed. It's almost as if I was never here before.

I'm so tired, I feel like I could sleep forever. In fact, for a moment the clean white sheets seem almost to be calling me. I stumble over and stop at the side of the bed, thinking back to the moment when I arrived at the B&B. All I wanted was somewhere to sleep, and now I'm exhausted. I guess it couldn't hurt to set my head down on the pillow, just for a moment, just to regain a little strength. I won't sleep, I'll just rest my tired, aching body. Besides, the sheets really *do* seem to be luring me down, and I can't help myself as I sit on the side of the bed and then roll onto the clean white expanse.

Heaven.

I could just close my eyes and sleep peacefully, and ignore the madness of the B&B and hope that somehow I wake up refreshed and alert in the morning. Maybe the whole situation will resolve itself without my input. Maybe I can just let the world take care of itself while I get some sleep.

No.

I can't do that.

And yet slowly, my eyes flicker shut. The bed is pulling me in.

Suddenly I hear a faint creaking sound. Startled, I sit bolt upright and see to my shock that Lloyd is standing at the foot of the bed, smiling at me.

"Don't get up!" he whispers, keeping his voice low as if he's worried about making too much noise. "You paid for the room, didn't you? Take a load off and catch forty winks."

"What are you doing in here?" I ask, feeling as if my heavy head is already pulling back toward the bed. "What -"

Before I can get another word out, I slump back down against the pillow. I want to get up, but my body feels so horrendously heavy. I immediately try to get up, but every bone is exhausted.

"What do you want?" I gasp.

I hear him stepping around the bed, but I can't even keep my eyes open.

"You've had such a long night," he purrs, his voice sounding like a lullaby. "I hope you'll enjoy your stay here at Castle Crown, Roberta. Breakfast is served downstairs in the basement room from seven until ten, or from eight until eleven on weekends. There's a tea and coffee machine available for use free of charge, along with a tray of biscuits and other snacks. I hope you'll feel free to help yourself if you get peckish during the night."

"Wait," I whisper, trying to sit up, only to feel an enormous weight holding me down against the bed. I try again, but I think I'm starting to fall asleep.

"We have one bathroom," he adds, slowly making his way around the bed, as if he wants to view me from all angles, "and that's on this floor. There's a shower *and* a bath, but please consider the needs of other guests in the morning and remember that we have twelve rooms here. I'm afraid it can get a little busy, but for your convenience there's a second toilet down in the basement, next to the boiler room."

"Stop," I gasp, forcing my eyes open and seeing Lloyd smiling down at me.

He stops at the bottom of the bed.

"If you have any further questions, or if there's anything you need at all, don't hesitate to come and knock. I'm here all day and all night, every single day, and I'll only be too happy to help. Castle Crown has been in my family for many years, and I consider it a matter of personal pride that every guest is made to feel welcome. We're like a little family here. But I should let you sleep now. As you'll no doubt have noticed, we have very clean, very bright white sheets. In fact, I believe they're the whitest money can buy."

He hesitates, staring down at the bed as if he's mesmerized.

"So white," he continues, his voice dwindling to barely more than a whisper. After a moment, he reaches down and runs a hand over the sheet. "So beautifully unspoiled. Not a drop spilled. Nothing but white."

"You're him," I stammer.

He glances at me. "I beg your pardon?"

"You're the one who..." I feel myself slipping away, but somehow I manage to find the strength to stay awake. "You're the one who kills those people," I continue. "You're the Snowman."

"Have you ever seen blood spilled on a pure

white sheet?" he continues. "You can't imagine it. I mean, you can try, but you can't fully understand unless you actually see it with your own two eyes. It's just not possible to describe the way the red starts to darken as it sinks into the fibers of the cotton, and the way it spread under the covers. I saw it twice when I was younger. First when I found Daddy, and then again when I found Mummy. And now, every time I see such beautiful white sheets, I can't help myself. I have to think about what they'd look like with blood seeping through the fabric, and then I have to think about whether..."

I gasp as I feel him running a finger along my left hand, up to my wrist.

"I can control myself most of the time," he says after a moment, his voice filled now with a sense of determination. "I'm not weak, you understand. I'm perfectly capable of keeping my urges in check. It's just that when the snow falls outside, and the whole world becomes white, there's nowhere left for me to look. The whiteness is all I can think about, and it starts burning through my chest. There's only one way to stop it... Fortunately, the snow always brings a stray visitor to the door. Always."

Suddenly he drops down to his knees, out of my field of vision. I try to tilt my head so I can see him, but I'm still too weak. I can feel his hand on my wrist, though, pressing harder as if he's trying to feel the veins and arteries. He's whispering something under his breath, too, although I can't quite make out the words.

Something about Mummy and Daddy.

Something about them leaving him all alone,

many years ago.

Finally managing to turn my head, I look over at the window and see flurries of snow coming down. The weather looks worse than ever, and for a moment it occurs to me that maybe this is what I deserve. I *should* die here, alone and hated, becoming the latest victim of the Snowman. I'm a liar and a thief, and this is what happens to liars and thieves.

"It won't hurt much," Lloyd gasps, as I feel his fingernails starting to slice through my flesh. "A little pain can produce a lot of beauty."

Blood is starting to dribble down to the palm of my hand now.

"These sheets are so white!" he hisses, his voice throbbing with anticipation. "I can't -"

Suddenly I let out a pained cry as I force myself to turn and roll off the bed. I slam down against the carpeted floor and then turn just in time to see Lloyd getting to his feet. I was about to go under, I was about to let him do whatever he wanted, but now my heart is pounding and I know I have to get the hell out of here. If I don't get away, I'll never find the suitcase and I'll never get the money back to the Chadwells.

"Are you fighting back?" Lloyd asks, already stepping around the bed. "That's noble. Futile, but noble. Besides, it's not like there's anywhere left for you to run to. Running was what brought you here in the first place, I believe?"

I roll under the bed and quickly emerge from the other side, but Lloyd steps back around to block my way again.

"Just sleep, Roberta," he continues, as I roll back under. "That's what this room is for. It's what this whole building is for. Most people fall asleep as soon as they arrive. You're the first guest who's ever left her room and explored the B&B. Perhaps guilt kept you awake."

He steps around the bed again. Realizing that I can't stay under here, I roll out the other side.

"You can't fight it," he adds, coming over to me yet again. "Others have tried before you. It's just not possible."

Letting out a grunt of anger, I throw myself forward, slamming into his legs and then scurrying to the door. Once I'm out on the landing, I race to the stairs but quickly stumble, crashing down and thudding to a halt next to the plant pot. The room's soporific effect is weaker already, but I'm still not free yet.

"Help!" I gasp, although I'm already starting to feel weak again. "Somebody! Anybody! Where are -"

Suddenly Lloyd steps into view at the top of the stairs. Panicked, I turn and start scrambling down, hurrying to the hallway and then over to the front door. When I try to turn the latch, however, I find that somehow it must have been locked. I try a couple more times, before realizing that I have to try the back door instead. I turn and run back past the foot of the stairs, just as Lloyd comes strolling down.

"Where do you think you're going?" he calls after me. "You're just tiring yourself out more and more. I'll only end up dragging you back up to the bed. Silly girl, you can't die until you're on the sheets. Try to remember that. We can't waste all that pretty blood."

Lunging at the back door, I find that here too the latch has somehow been locked. I pull frantically, trying to find some way out, before turning as I hear footsteps getting closer.

"Help me!" I shout, convinced that one of the others has to hear me, but after a moment I turn and race down the stairs that lead to the basement. I trip halfway, falling forward and tumbling to the bottom. I land hard, cracking something in my left shoulder, but at least the pain forces me awake.

There's no sign of anyone down here, so I run to the boiler room and pull the door open. Once I'm inside, there's no time to search for a light-switch, so I stumble through the darkness and try to find the stairs. It takes a moment, but finally I grab hold of the railing, and -

Suddenly the lights flicker on above me.

I turn, just as Lloyd grabs my collar and slams me against the wall. The impact is strong enough to force the air from my lungs and send the back of my head thudding against the breeze-blocks. He quickly pushes me down onto the dusty concrete floor, leaving me gasping as I feel a sharp pain in my chest. When I try to breathe, I feel as if I can only fill up a tiny portion of my lungs at a time.

"I must admit," Lloyd says as he comes closer and stops to tower over me, "I was a little surprised when I looked in your suitcase. That's a lot of cash you're carrying around in there, Roberta. So much, in fact, that I can't in all honesty believe that you're completely on the level. You're hiding something. Don't worry, though. I'm not going to waste my time trying to figure out what you did or where you come from. None of that matters. All that matters is that you're here, and that you're guilty, and that yet again I found someone to come through the front door on a cold, snowy night. Funny how that always works out, isn't it?"

Rolling onto my back, I feel a sharp pain slicing through my chest. I think I might have fractured a couple or ribs.

"Of course," he adds, "I usually open the front door to welcome new guests. But since you chose to explore a little, I didn't even have to do that this time. It really has been a long and strange night, hasn't it?"

Suddenly Lloyd reaches down and tucks something into the upper-left breast pocket of my uniform.

"The Castle Crown business card," he explains, as he steps over me. "Not many people find it. You should consider yourself lucky."

I roll onto my other side and watch as he heads over to a table in the corner. My suitcase is open on the table, and it's clear that he's been going through my things. After a moment, however, he picks up a rusty old hammer.

"It's funny how the world works, isn't it?" he continues, seemingly lost in thought for a moment as he examines the hammer's head. "Souls in need invariably get what they want, even if it's not what they *think* they want. The tectonic plates of the universe simply shift beneath their feet, delivering them to wherever they should be. And that's how, I guess, a guilty little girl on the run ends up on the steps outside my humble home."

He smiles. "Now you get to become one of my pet ghosts."

"*Your* ghosts?" I stammer, wincing with pain as I try to drag myself away.

"I was shocked when it first happened," he replies. "The first time I killed one of my guests, I dragged her body a long way from the building, so that I wouldn't be suspected. Then I saw hints of her presence when I got back. As I killed more and more over the years, I became increasingly certain that the souls of my victim were somehow becoming stuck here. I didn't mind. They weren't disruptive, at least not until I killed Mrs. Denham. Three months later, after the police had given up trying to find her, I was shocked by the sudden arrival of her husband. He didn't suspect me of anything, of course. He simply needed somewhere to stay while he poked around. And then, rather poetically, more snow came and I killed him, and then I had both their ghosts around me."

"Ghosts aren't real!" I hiss, forcing myself to sit up. Looking around, I try to spot something I can use as a weapon. I need to buy a little time. "They can't be! You're just crazy!"

"If they're not real, who have you been talking to tonight? Apart from me, at least."

"They weren't ghosts," I stammer, trying to drag myself toward one of the tables.

"Their dead bodies would surely disagree."

"They can't be ghosts," I whisper, trying to take slow, careful breaths. "It's not possible."

"Major Denham's death was when the problems

started," he continues. "His ghost and his wife's ghost found one another and began to mingle. Evidently this set off some kind of chain reaction, and soon all the ghosts here at Castle Crown became aware of one another. At first, I thought it was the end of me, but over time they simply began to socialize. They were haunting each other, instead of haunting me! All except the first, Elizabeth, who seemed scared of the rest, but she just lurks on the top floor. There were some unforeseen side-effects of this arrangement, though. One of which was that sometimes, in this house at least, the perspective of the living becomes affected by the needs of the dead. Events occasionally get stuck in little loops here, as I'm sure you've noticed by now. Even the lives of the living can become entangled in the ghosts' way of doing things."

I'm almost at the table, but my lungs are screaming with pain. I open my mouth to tell Lloyd that he's crazy, but suddenly I hear footsteps racing across the ceiling directly above us.

"Help!" I gasp, but I'm in too much pain to raise my voice about a faint whisper. "Please..."

I reach a trembling hand up toward the beams.

"Such a busy house," Lloyd continues, stepping closer to me. "Don't worry. I'm going to make this very easy for you. I'll simply knock you out and take you back to your room, and then I'll do what I do to all my guests. And then, once your body has been disposed of, you'll take your place with the rest of them. You'll be quite happy, doing the same thing over and over again. Really, you should be thanking me. I'm going to let you stay here forever, and all you have to do in return is bleed a little over my nice white sheets."

"Go to hell!" I hiss, trying to kick his ankles.

He laughs.

"Go to hell!" I shout, trying but failing to get to my feet.

"I'm sure your sheet will go nicely with my collection," he continues.

"What collection?" I ask.

"Haven't you seen it yet?"

He looks past me. Turning, I'm shocked to see several white bed-sheets pinned against the farthest wall, each with its own distinctive patch of dried blood. Some of the sheets look much older than others. Some have brownish, faded stains, while others look more recent. There are six in total, and for a moment I stare at them in horror.

Suddenly I'm grabbed from behind. Lloyd puts an arm around my neck and swings me around, slamming me against the wall.

"You'll be number seven!" he hisses into my ear. "Daddy and Mummy were one and two. Then came Elizabeth, Matilda, Major and Mrs. Denham... And now you!"

I try to pull free, but he squeezes my neck even tighter.

"Mummy and Daddy should never have left me alone!" he hisses into my ear. "I was just a boy! I learned to manage, though! I think I turned out just fine!"

I gasp, trying to get free, but he's choking me.

"The police will be looking for the Snowman out there!" he continues. "All the while, they'll never -"

Before he can finish, I elbow him hard in the ribs, sending him stumbling back. Seizing my chance, I turn and try to run toward the steps, only for Lloyd to grab my ankle and drag me down. Slamming against the concrete, I swing around and kick him hard in the face, and then I try again to reach the steps. The pain in my ribs is intense, holding me back, but finally I'm able to grab the edge of the first step and start hauling myself up. Only -

Suddenly the hammer's handle slams into the back of my head, sending me back down onto my knees. I fall forward, landing against the side of one of the tables, and for a moment my vision is blurred. After blinking several times, I'm surprised to see my coffee mug from earlier. It's on the edge of the table, resting exactly where I left it when I was down here in the boiler room before.

"Like I told you," Lloyd says calmly, stepping up behind me, "you can't run. Even if you try, you'll only end up right back here. This is your destiny."

"Maybe," I gasp, reaching out and grabbing the mug as I hear Lloyd picking up the hammer. "And maybe this is yours."

With that, I get to my feet and swing the mug at him, slamming it against the side of his head. The mug immediately breaks, and Lloyd steps back with a shocked look on his face.

"What's -"

He stares at the broken mug in my hands. For a

moment, I actually think he might be about to pass out, but then slowly a smile spreads across his lips.

"Is that your best effort?" he asks, as blood starts dribbling from a wound on his temple. "Oh dear. Did you think you could -"

Before he can get another word out, I swing the mug's broken section at his head, hitting him again. This time, he laughs as he steps back.

"Oh dear," he continues, as I try to get my breath back. "You don't really have it in you, do you? You're not the killing type."

I take a series of snatched breaths, trying to work up the strength to strike him again.

"Go on," he says, wiping tears of mirth from his eyes. "I'm a good sport, so I'll give you a fair chance. Try one more time. Really whack me as hard as you can."

I strengthen my grip on the broken mug.

"Use every ounce of hatred in your body," he continues, and now his smile is fading. "Go on. Try to knock me out. Do you worst."

I swing again, and this time I hit him even harder, sending him thudding back against one of the support posts. He stares at me for a moment, with more and more blood flowing down his face, and then he tries to say something before finally slumping to the ground.

I reach down and grab the hammer, which slipped from his hand when he fell, and then I hold it up, ready to defend myself if he attacks again. My heart is pounding, but Lloyd's eyes are wide open and there's no sign of movement. I whacked him hard with the mug, as hard as I could manage, and I think finally I stopped him.

Still, I wait a couple of minutes, just in case he stirs. Finally, feeling another burst of pain in my ribs, I realize it's over.

"Thanks for the stay," I whisper, limping past his body and heading over to the table in the corner, where my suitcase has been left with its lid wide open.

I glance over my shoulder to make doubly sure that Lloyd hasn't moved, and then I quickly check that all the money is still in the suitcase. Once I'm sure that I have what I need, I close the lid and pull the zip around, and then I haul the suitcase off the table and turn to look at Lloyd again. There's a fair amount of blood pooled beside his head now, and his dead eyes are still staring up toward the basement's low wooden ceiling.

"I'm sorry I had to do that," I tell him, feeling a shudder pass through my chest as I realize that I actually killed him. When I arrived at the B&B, I was a thief. Now I've killed someone. Sure, it was self-defense, but that doesn't make me feel any better. I'm still a killer. I guess that'll be one more thing for me to deal with once this insane night is over. "I'll let someone know to come clean up the mess."

Figuring that I finally need to get out of here, I turn and start hauling the suitcase toward the door. My arms are aching, but I know I just have to keep going. Letting out a gasp, I feel the suitcase catch on a crack in the floor, so I have to pull extra hard, and I swear I feel like I might be about to collapse.

Suddenly I hear someone laughing.

I turn, just as Lloyd slams the mug's broken handle against the side of my head, sending me crashing back down to the ground.

"Did you really think it was that easy?" he asks, tossing the handle aside before picking up hammer and stepping closer, until he's towering over me. "Honestly? A smack on the side of the head with an old mug, and you thought you'd killed me? It was all I could do to keep from laughing after I fell."

"Please," I stammer, as he raises the hammer. "Don't do this!"

"You're not a killer!" he sneers, as his grin widens. "Face it, Bobbie. You don't have it in you. You don't have the guts. Even when I presented you with an open goal, you couldn't strike the fatal blow. I suppose you're just not that kind of person."

With that, he raises the hammer.

"Please don't kill me!" I whimper, as tears start streaming down my face. "I have to take the money back!"

"You couldn't kill me," he continues with a chuckle, "not even to save your own life. You don't have what it takes, not in your heart. You're just not a -"

Suddenly the end of an iron poker slices through the ceiling and straight down into the top of his head, quickly bursting out through his mouth. He freezes, staring straight at me with shocked eyes as blood starts dribbling freely from his lips. The poker's tip starts shuddering, as if it's being wiggled around, and after a moment it slides back up and out the top of his head, and it disappears back through the hole in the ceiling.

Lloyd stays in place for a moment, still staring at me, still holding the hammer, as the dribble of blood becomes a torrent that rushes from his mouth. Finally he slumps forward, and I just manage to roll out of the way in time as he lands hard next to me. This time, his head cracks against the concrete floor, and I'm left staring at the bloody hole where the iron poker miraculously slid straight through his brain.

"Great!" I hear my own voice hiss in the room above, followed by a metal bump and then the sound of several stumbling footsteps.

Staying completely still next to Lloyd's corpse, barely even daring to breathe, I listen to myself moving about in the office. I remember being up there earlier, and I remember trying to use the iron poker as a kind of walking stick. I remember the poker's tip suddenly breaking through the floorboards and sliding down, and I remember having to pull it back up. I *don't* remember seeing blood on the tip, but I guess I was too busy freezing in my wet clothes at the time.

For the next few minutes, too exhausted to move a muscle, I simply stay flat on my back and listen to myself moving about up there. Finally, however, I hear another noise.

A knock on the door.

"Oh, go away," I hear myself muttering in the room above.

A moment later, there's another knock.

"Shut up!" I hear myself hiss. "Quiet! You'll wake them!"

I hear myself heading out into the hallway, and a

few seconds later I hear the front door swinging open. I remember that exact moment. It's when the madness looped around for the first time and began to happen all over again. Right now, up there, the bandaged version of me is staring in shock at the version of me that's out in the snow.

It's all starting again.

Maybe it's never going to stop, but I have to try.

Hauling myself up, I look down at Lloyd one more time and see that this time he's absolutely, well and truly, positively dead. I guess I killed him hours ago, at the crucial moment, but I never realized until just now. Figuring that I can panic later, I grab the suitcase and haul it back over to the door, before dragging it out into the hallway. Just as I'm about to pull the door shut, however, I find myself face-to-face with Matilda and the Denhams.

"Is he in there?" Matilda asks calmly.

"We remember," Mrs. Denham adds. "What he did to us."

"I don't know how we forgot," Matilda whispers, "but we remember now."

I hesitate for a moment, before stepping aside. I watch as they head into the boiler room, and a moment later I hear a whimpering voice in the darkness. It's Lloyd, but not as an adult. It's the voice of a young boy.

"What are you going to do to him?" I ask.

Matilda stops in the doorway, behind the others, and turns to me.

"He's damaged," I explain, trying not to panic. "I know he did awful, awful things, but when he was a

189

kid... I know that's no excuse, but at least you can try to understand. I've been in a similar situation. I know what it's like to be young and alone, and to make a terrible choice."

I wait for an answer, but she simply stares at me as Lloyd's ghost continues to whimper in the room behind her.

"Please," I continue, "don't -"

Suddenly Matilda slams the door shut in my face, and Lloyd lets out another, even more pained cry. I take a step back, before realizing I don't want to hear any more of this. Turning, I head toward the stairs, only to see that the final ghost – the timid woman who kept avoiding me – is coming down. She glances at me briefly as she passes, but she doesn't say anything. Instead, she simply makes her way to the door and pushes it open before slipping inside to join the others.

For a moment, I can hear Lloyd begging them to leave him alone. Somehow, I don't think they'll show him any mercy.

And then the door slams shut again, with enough force to rattle the frame.

EPILOGUE

THERE'S STILL A LOT of snow coming down. Somehow, despite everything that happened to me tonight, it's still only 10pm. I guess the B&B spat me back out at the very start of the evening.

Thanks to my throbbing ankle and my painful hip and my fractured ribs, not to mention several other little cuts and scratches that I never even got around to mentioning, it takes me almost an hour to lug my suitcase through the uncleared streets. I almost give up a couple of times, but deep down I know I have to keep going. I have a train to catch. I have to go home and face the music for what I did.

When I finally reach Canterbury East station, I find that it's pretty much deserted. I check the board and see that the next train back to Ashford leaves in about one hours' time, which means I've got a long wait on the cold platform. Still, I guess that'll give me time to think about what I'm going to say when I walk through the door, and what I'll say to the police. I only spent about £200 of the money, so I can give most of the £26,000 straight back. I know that won't be enough to undo the damage, but at least it's a start.

What happens to me after that is out of my control, but I'll take my punishment. I've got to admit, though... I wish I'd remembered to throw that plant out the window before I left the B&B.

Stopping at the waiting room's locked door, I lean back against the wall and try to get my breath back. At first, I listen to the sound of the quiet city, but after a moment I realize I can see a couple of lights in the distance, moving through the streets. I guess the night-watch team is still out, still trying to keep the people of Canterbury safe. I guess they were ghosts too, each of them the father or mother of one of the Snowman's victims. Maybe they'll find peace now that Lloyd is finally dead. The Snowman's reign of terror is over.

Suddenly I hear a voice nearby. I turn, looking toward the phone-box, and I freeze as soon as I see the girl who's in there.

It's me.

Or rather, it's an earlier version of me, calling B&B numbers from the phone book in a desperate last-minute attempt to find a room. She has her back to me, and I can just about make out her voice in the cold night air.

I remember this.

"Okay, thank you," I hear her saying, before she puts the phone back on the hook. Next, I hear her sorting through her change, and then she makes another call.

This happened earlier.

I watch for a few more minutes, poised to duck back into the shadows in case she happens to glance this way, but she seems utterly focused on making more calls. Her suitcase is propped next to her, and I can't help thinking back to how scared and lost I felt when I was in that phone-box. I was panicking, and I was exhausted, and all I could think about was the fact that I had to keep running.

She finishes another call and turns to the next page in the phone book. Only a couple more numbers left, and none of them will have room. And then -

Pausing, I suddenly remember the card in my pocket. Taking it out, I see that it shows a faded drawing of the Castle Crown B&B, along with a phone number. Lloyd tucked this card into my pocket earlier, but I remember seeing one even before that, when I was in the phone-box. Without even thinking, I start making my way toward the earlier version of me, listening as she makes a couple more calls. Finally I'm right behind her, so close that I can see her reflection in the phone's glass panel.

And she could see mine, if she just happened to look this way.

"That's fine," she says as she finishes yet another call. "I'm sorry to have bothered you."

She sets the phone down, and then she simply looks at the phone book for a moment. A drop of muddy snow falls onto the patch of skin just behind her ear. She wipes it away, leaving a small dollop behind. Suddenly remembering this moment, I realize it's the point at which I finished calling all the names in the book without any luck. I hesitate for a few seconds, before remembering exactly how I found the B&B's card. I look down, but there's no card on the ground, and I realize what I have to do.

Stepping back, I let the card fall from my hand, and I watch as it lands on the snow right outside the door.

Suddenly the earlier version of me pushes the door open. Letting out a faint, barely audible gasp, I step back into the shadows and watch as she stops again. She reaches down and picks up the card, staring at it for a moment before putting some more coins into the phone and trying to call the Castle Crown.

Of course, nobody will pick up.

Finally she heads off, dragging her suitcase through the snow, while tucking the card into her pocket. She's going to go knock on the B&B's door, and a bandaged woman will answer, and then she'll go inside and all the madness will begin again. I could warn her, I could call out and save her the trouble, but instead I stay quiet and watch as she disappears into the distance. She's not exactly going to get the night's rest she's after, but I think this needed to happen. Besides, if I start thinking about the details of this night, I think I might just lose my mind.

Finally, one hour later, I step on-board the train that'll take me home.

B&B

AMY CROSS

Also by Amy Cross

The Curse of Wetherley House

"If you walk through that door, Evil Mary will get you."

When she agrees to visit a supposedly haunted house with an old friend, Rosie assumes she'll encounter nothing more scary than a few creaks and bumps in the night. Even the legend of Evil Mary doesn't put her off. After all, she knows ghosts aren't real. But when Mary makes her first appearance, Rosie realizes she might already be trapped.

For more than a century, Wetherley House has been cursed. A horrific encounter on a remote road in the late 1800's has already caused a chain of misery and pain for all those who live at the house. Wetherley House was abandoned long ago, after a terrible discovery in the basement, something has remained undetected within its room. And even the local children know that Evil Mary waits in the house for anyone foolish enough to walk through the front door.

Before long, Rosie realizes that her entire life has been defined by the spirit of a woman who died in agony. Can she become the first person to escape Evil Mary, or will she fall victim to the same fate as the house's other occupants?

Also by Amy Cross

The Ghosts of Hexley Airport

Ten years ago, more than two hundred people died in a horrific plane crash at Hexley Airport.

Today, some say their ghosts still haunt the terminal building.

When she starts her new job at the airport, working a night shift as part of the security team, Casey assumes the stories about the place can't be true. Even when she has a strange encounter in a deserted part of the departure hall, she's certain that ghosts aren't real.

Soon, however, she's forced to face the truth. Not only is there something haunting the airport's buildings and tarmac, but a sinister force is working behind the scenes to replicate the circumstances of the original accident. And as a snowstorm moves in, Hexley Airport looks set to witness yet another disaster.

Printed in Great Britain
by Amazon

81131248R00120